DEATH IN
FANCY DRESS

By JEFFERSON FARJEON

Author of *Thirteen Guests* and *Mystery in White*

THE BOBBS-MERRILL COMPANY
PUBLISHERS

INDIANAPOLIS   NEW YORK

FIRST EDITION

Printed in the United States of America

PRINTED AND BOUND BY
BRAUNWORTH & CO, INC.
BUILDERS OF BOOKS
BRIDGEPORT. CONN.

CONTENTS

DEATH IN FANCY DRESS

NINE P.M.

THERE is a theory, which some people find harder and
harder to refute, that the world is mad. Yet who
among us can definitely prove or disprove this asser-
tion? Madness, often enough, is merely a relative
term, and the lunatic of yesterday may be the sage of
today, while the sage of today may become the lunatic
of tomorrow. There appears as yet no central point to
sanity, unless it resides in the elusive seed of human
happiness, and happiness is as difficult to define as
madness itself.

But if those who take an uncomplimentary view of
the world's condition wish to reinforce their opinion
they can do so once a year, at least, by purchasing a
ticket for the Chelsea Arts Ball at the Albert Hall.
Here our search for happiness takes the strangest
form. From 10:00 P.M. till 5:00 A.M. sober folk dis-
card their sobriety, flinging themselves into queer costumes and queerer mental attitudes in an attempt to
forget the humdrum of existence. For seven hours

they play this game, thumbing their noses at Fate, and laughing at Reality.

Yet Fate stalks in their midst, and Reality beats in their hearts. For it is only a game, this attempt to escape from the humdrum, and the underlying pathos shatters criticism. The real story of that man over there is not in his bandit costume; it is on the Stock Exchange, among considerably duller forms and figures. That elderly gentleman behind him, watching the dancers revolve round the vast dancing space, has nothing to do with the gaily-lined Venetian cloak he is wearing; he is wasting away with disease, trying to warm cold fingers in a fading fire. The beautiful, sparsely-clad nymph who floats dreamily by and throws him a little smile (or so he pretends) will be serving, tomorrow, in a West End shop. That coy blonde with deep frank bosoms is speeding despairingly toward sixty.

Others, more fortunate, do receive a definite fillip to the momentary happiness they have brought with them from outside. The lights, the color, the music, all on the most elaborate and most magnificent scale, add to their natural buoyancy of spirit, and these true lovers who mingle with the sensualist and the cynic find in the Albert Hall an almost overpowering fulfilment of an exciting dream. But all possess stories of one kind or another which have their center elsewhere, and as the great ballroom revolves with its comedy and tragedy, its light and its shade, some of the stories are suspended, and some go on.

Henry Brown regarded his half-shaved face in the little mirror hanging by his bed. He regarded it with disapproval, almost with panic. It looked worried when it ought to have looked gay, for this was to be a night of nights, an occasion of high adventure and rare audacity, and, if he did not begin in the right mood, in which kind of a mood would he end? He forced a smile into his strained features. "This is *fun!*" he assured himself, overdoing the confidence. His smile did nothing to compose his agitated mind.

He turned from the mirror to the window. The window-glass was obscured by a dark, worn blind. The cord was off the blind and you had to give the bottom a careful tug to get it up. Not a hard tug. If you did that something disastrous happened and the blind stayed down for days. A soft, delicate tug. . . . He gave a soft, delicate tug. The blind shot up with a violent snap, snarled round the top roller, and became wedged. Now it would stay up for days.

"Damn!" muttered Henry Brown.

Life was very difficult.

With the blind up he feared that everybody would see in, and he was not in a condition to be viewed.

Almost immediately, however, he realized that he had no need to worry about his visibility. No one could see in if he himself could not see out. A thick fog hung outside the window, a brooding, yellow, impenetrable curtain. It had been threatening all day. The morning paper had predicted it, the evening wireless had confirmed it, and here it was, adding fresh trouble to the occasion. Henry's mind jerked from one trial to another, and the lines on his rather tired face deepened.

"Fog!" he grunted. "That's a nice thing! How am I going to *get* to the blessed place?" Then another thought struck him. "Yes, and what happens if I *can't?*"

For a brief instant the possibility of not getting there brightened, surprisingly, his horizon. He recognized that although he had planned and plotted to get there, and had scraped and saved to get there, he also dreaded getting there; and no one could call you a funk, could they, for failing to turn up at a place you could not reach! If this particular place could not be reached—if the busses were at a standstill and the taxis were sprawling across the pavement—then Henry Brown would be forced to spend the evening at home, and nobody would ever see him in the ridiculous costume that lay on his bed waiting for his insufficient body. A loose velvet jacket of unfamiliar shape.

Strange, hugely-checked slacks. An enormous flowing blue tie. A vast red sash. Or was the tie the sash, and the sash the tie? And above all, in every sense, a mammoth beret. Not the happy beret of a Borotra, but an endless expanse of dark ribbed stuff that flowed over the side of your head almost down to your neck, giving you the feeling that you were in deep mourning for a pancake. It was this Gargantuan headgear that had first upset Henry's morale and that now made him momentarily bless the fog.

The moment passed, however. Henry was even more afraid of fear than of the thing he feared. He did not possess a first-class mind, but it was good enough to recognize the spuriousness of his excuses. And there was, in addition, the financial side of the question to strengthen his resolve and to urge him forward. The hiring of the costume had cost half a guinea, paid in advance. The paid in advance was important. It meant that you could not get the money back again. Then the ticket for the Albert Hall had cost another thirty-one and six. You saved ten-and-six by purchasing it hazardously before the actual day. Happily the ticket included supper, so you could be sure of getting something definite for your outlay. Then, again, there was a manicure. Henry had thought a lot about the manicure. It was not likely that his small hand would be noticed in the vastness of the

Albert Hall, but somehow or other the manicure had
seemed necessary; though not a pedicure. He had
never been manicured before, and he had suffered
acutely when the manicurist had taken his unattractive
hand into her pretty one and had replied to his muttered apologies that she had seen worse. Two shillings,
that suffering had cost, with sixpence for the girl.
That raised the damage to date up to £2 4s. 6d. Almost a week's pay! No, dammit, you couldn't allow
yourself to waste so much as that!

There was something deeper than purse or pride,
however, that drew Henry back into the current of
terrifying desire. It was the stirring possibility of
adventure and romance. Not that adventure and
romance were likely to come his way, for people of
his timid type rarely attract them. Still—you never
knew, did you? Some girl or other *might* smile at him
in the crowd, and he *might* smile back. He might even
have the courage to ask her for a dance. Particularly
if wine were included in the supper! You never *knew,*
did you?

He returned determinedly to his shaving. He could
wake up on the morrow resigned to the knowledge that
adventure had not come his way, but he would wake
up in a torment of distraction, he was convinced, if
through eleventh hour funk he failed to resolve the
agonizing question!

His shaving complete, he felt his chin. The utter smoothness of it comforted him. No barber could have shaved him closer for sixpence. And he had not cut himself.

Then, taking a breath, he tackled the strange garments on the bed.

His pants and his vest, as he stood in them before the plunge, had never seemed so dear to him. They were like a familiar home about to be obliterated. He decided not to look at himself during the obliterating process, for to watch the metamorphosis bit by bit would be too unnerving. When the transformation was accomplished and he regarded himself in the mirror, the shock was almost more than he could bear. He discovered, to his dismay, that he had dared to hope.

"Do you mean to tell me," he cried aloud to his reflection, "that any girl is going to dance with *that?*"

He seized the flowing beret from his head and hurled it to the ground. Then he picked it up again.

"Silly ass!" he growled at himself. "You'd think a girl was all I was going for!"

Possibly it was.

He glanced at the clock on the mantelpiece. A quarter past nine. That was a nuisance. He wished it had been later. The ball didn't start till ten, and you'd look a fool if you got there earlier. On the other hand,

you didn't want to waste any of it by getting there late.
And, of course, the fog would mean slow traveling.

"Five minutes—I'll wait five minutes," he decided.
What could he do to fill out five minutes?

All at once he thought of it. Money! Whew, he
might have gone without any! His forehead perspired
at the ghastly idea. How much did one take? Just
enough for the fare there and back? Or a shilling or
two over, in case of accidents? "I suppose wine *is*
included?" he reflected. "But suppose it isn't? Will I
want any?" He rarely took wine. For one reason, he
could not afford it, and for another, a very little went
a long way. "No, I won't want any," he settled it.
"This is costing me quite enough as it is." Then into
Henry's wavering mind came a sudden startling vision.
It had no right to come, but it did. He saw himself
sitting at a little supper table in a secluded corner.
Opposite was a girl of dazzling loveliness. Her cheeks
were flushed, but her bare shoulders were white, with
tiny shadowy pools in the contours. He saw them as
distinctly as that. "I've lost my party," she was laughing. "One always does at the Chelsea Arts. Do you
mind?"

He came out of the vision with a wrench. His forehead was damper now than ever. "Steady!" he muttered to himself. "You're not drunk yet, you know!"
He was. With excitement.

He went to the box where he kept his money. His fingers trembled slightly as he unlocked it. The box contained four one-pound notes. Apart from the twelve-and-sixpence in silver which still lay on his bed, these four pound notes were all the wealth he possessed in the world. He began to lock the box. Then quickly, to cheat his intelligence, he unlocked it again and seized the notes. "Just in case," he said aloud.

Putting the empty box away, and fighting against a sensation of theft, he began to slip the notes in his trouser pocket. The notes slid nakedly over the loose, grotesque material. He discovered to his dismay that his costume did not possess any trouser pockets. The only pockets he could find were two wide ones, painfully obvious, on either side of the velvet jacket. A pickpocket could slip his hand into them with the utmost ease.

"That's done it!" thought Henry.

But the notion of leaving the notes at home because he did not know where to carry them shamed him. It suggested that he was allowing circumstances to steer his course, when tonight he was in a mood to steer circumstances. He wondered whether they would be safe in his beret. There was room in the beret for the whole Mint! Then all at once he found his solution. He took off his black shoes, folded the notes, and put two in each shoe. When he had the shoes on again they tickled his soles pleasantly, giving him an odd rich feeling.

The silver had to take its chance in one of the jacket pockets.

He glanced at the clock again. Twenty past nine. Good! Just right!

"Now I'm really off," he said.

He walked to the door and listened. He wanted to get out of the house without being seen. He had put on his overcoat, but the loud slacks were not obliterated. They shouted for nine inches below where the overcoat ended.

Hearing no one, he turned the door handle softly and peeped out into the passage. Empty. Good again! But the peeling walls seemed to have eyes that bored into his soul and questioned it. He turned, without knowing why, and took a last look at his room. He felt as though he were saying good-by to himself.

It has been indicated that as yet there was no particular girl in Henry Brown's life, or in his mind. Girl existed for him in the abstract, and it was to be the mission of the Albert Hall to translate the abstract into material terms. But if, while he had struggled with his reflection in his looking-glass, he could have seen the reflection of Dorothy Shannon in another, daintier mirror, he might have gone to the Chelsea Arts Ball already conquered.

The reflection of Dorothy Shannon was very different from that of Henry Brown. It was wholly satisfactory. From the topmost hair of her auburn crop down to the tips of her golden shoes, she was five-foot-eight of sheer loveliness. In the frankly-expressed opinion of her parents she would easily stand out as the most beautiful sight in the whole of the hall. She was somewhat inclined to this view herself. It was temporary excitement, however, rather than natural vanity that made her hopeful; and her brother Conrad, on the other hand, betrayed a less flattering perspicacity.

"Yes, you look topping, Sis," he admitted, popping his head in through her door, "but don't run away with any high-falutin' ideas about yourself. You'll be utterly lost in the crowd, you know."

"*You* won't!" retorted Dorothy, with conviction. "And, of course, don't trouble to knock when you enter a lady's bedroom!"

Conrad grinned. He had seen to it that he himself would not be lost in the crowd. At the previous New Year's Ball he had been utterly lost as a pirate—in company with countless other pirates—but this year he had vowed that, for better or worse, he *would* be noticed, and the head that had popped in so unceremoniously through his sister's door was completely gold. Completely gold, also, was the rest of him. The gilding process had cost him considerable time and agony; but there are strange occasions in life, and this was one of them, when fools stand out where ·wise men cease to shine; and, although Conrad did not know it, there was something oddly artistic about his queer appearance. He looked like a golden Grecian statue, of which perhaps the most remarkable part was the curly, gold-clogged hair.

"Do go away," pleaded Dorothy, as he lingered.

"There's nowhere to go to," he answered gloomily. "Nowhere peaceful, I mean. Father's swearing at his wig—you'd think the whole of Cosmos depended upon its set—and Mother's running around him picking up the things he drops, and this house, once so sweet and calm, is a cauldron of despair." He paused and regarded his sister critically. "Of course, I suppose you are aware that you don't look a bit like Du Barry——"

"Oh, *don't* I?" interrupted Dorothy, and thrust an old copy of a theatrical journal toward him. It was open at a full-page picture of Annie Ahlers on which she had based her conception. "Tell me where I'm wrong?"

"Yes, you look like *that*," he agreed, "but that's out of a musical show, and musical shows aren't history. The Du Barry in the play, I remember, became the mistress of a handsome and attractive French monarch, but the historical Du Barry—the *real* Du Barry—attached herself to a Louis XV who was entering senile decay, so she must have been a nasty, filthy sort of person. Fact. Listen!" He opened a fat book he had brought with him and read: " 'When Du Barry met the King of France he was already, at sixty years of age, in his dotage of shame.' So, to avoid historical inaccuracy, my dear, look out for slobbering old boys tonight! Yes, and you want to have some dirty cracks ready for 'em, too. Listen again; 'Her piquant if vulgar wit amused the worn-out dotard.' "

"How *do* you expect me to get on while you babble?" she groaned.

"And you had a most horrible end," continued the gilded youth, irrepressibly. "I trust it is not prophetic. You sneaked over to London to sell your jewels, and when you got back to France you were arrested for wasting treasures of State, and you were guillotined on December 7, 1793. Voilà!"

"Are you suggesting that I shall be guillotined at the Albert Hall?" inquired Dorothy.

"Oh, I don't expect it will be quite as bad as that," answered Conrad, "but it might be wise to remember that Du Barry's always a bit of a Jonah. You'd have been safer as Little Miss Muffit. Hallo! Bell! Would that be Harold?"

"If it is, for God's sake go down and give him his shock!" she burst out.

"Good notion," he nodded. "I will! The poor lad's got to get it over. Exit the Golden Statue." He turned, then paused to add, "By the way, I rather like the idea of an M.P. for a brother-in-law. What's the betting Harold proposes tonight?"

He vanished. Dorothy stared after him indignantly. As she removed her eyes back to the mirror, however, she could not deny that he was probably right. "Though that does not mean," she informed her reflection, "that I shall accept the proposal!"

Passing his parents' bedroom on his way down to the hall, Conrad found the door ajar, and stopped to listen. He loved hearing other people's conversations, not to make use of them, but just for the sheer fun of it. They generally sounded idiotic. And then it was amusing trying to guess. You pass two tongue-wagging women in Oxford Street and one of them is saying: "My dear, he *did!* And before everybody!" Did what? Or in a bus: "From the top to the bottom, and then up and along." Knitting or diving? Once at a concert, during Tschaikovsky's *Pathetic Symphony,* he had bent forward to learn musical secrets from a couple of white-haired professors in the row ahead of him, and had found them comparing notes as to the best way to cook onions. . . .

Now, through the crack of the slightly-open bedroom door, came the voices of his parents.

"Wonder if that's Harold?"

"Would you hold your head a little higher, dear?"

"Well, I am. It's a bit thoughtless of him getting here so early."

"No, no, not as high as that!"

"Eh? I hope one of us is ready."

"Well, if not, he'll just have to wait. Now, then, look at yourself. Is that any better?"

"We don't want him to wait! He's—yes, much better. But, you know, something's still wrong with the wig. Doesn't it hang down lower on one side than the other?"

"If it does, I expect it's supposed to." (The listener in the passage chuckled. Poor old Mother!) "I like your buckles." (The listener chuckled again. The subtle praise that turneth away wrath!)

"Eh? Do you? Yes, not bad. I suppose men *did* wear red heels in those days? Damn silly. Somebody ought to go down. Where's Conrad?"

"Don't *worry*, dear! It really won't hurt Harold to wait two minutes."

"He's not going to wait! Call Conrad!"

"He mayn't be dressed."

"Then he ought to be dressed." ("Why? *He's* not," reflected Conrad.) "Yes, damn it, it does hang lower!

Anyway, you'd better find out. What about a patch?
Did Charles II wear a patch?"

Conrad retreated a few steps, then advanced again
loudly. He was passing the bedroom door as his
mother looked out.

"Go down, dear!" she whispered hoarsely. "We
think that's Harold!"

"Just on my way," answered Conrad airily.

Something suddenly smote his soul, causing him to
pause. Something about his mother. He wondered
what it was. She wasn't half ready herself. Of course
that didn't really matter, for although the ball started
officially at ten it went on till five next morning, and
to miss a dance or two was no catastrophe. Some
people didn't turn up till just before midnight. The
only real urgency resided in one's own impatience.
Still. . . .

"You haven't got very far with your own glad
rags," he commented, the hard gaiety momentarily
departing from his voice.

She felt vaguely surprised, and vaguely pleased. It
was rather nice, somehow, his saying that. She had not
even commenced to put on her fancy costume, that of
a china shepherdess with a long crook, although she
was absent-mindedly holding the crook. The crook
seemed to accentuate her deshabille, like a sword in
the hand of a naked soldier. Mrs. Shannon was not

naked, but her deshabille was so frank that Conrad found himself striving not to be worried by it. He was never really comfortable in the presence of too much bosom. It was not his own discomfort, however, but his mother's, that concerned him now. She had given a hand to everybody during the hectic dressing period, but who had given her a hand?

"Mary!" came a shout from the bedroom. Charles II was in difficulties again. "Snuff! What about snuff?"

Mrs. Shannon vanished back into the bedroom, and Conrad completed his interrupted journey to the hall below.

A rather massive man of thirty looked up as he came round the final bend of the staircase.

"Good God!" exclaimed the rather massive man, involuntarily. "What's this? The Gold Standard?"

Harold Lankester had himself played for safety, and was unimpeachable, if somewhat heavy, as a Russian dancer.

"Please be a little more parliamentary in your language," replied Conrad solemnly. "However, I'm glad you like it."

"Thanks for the information," smiled Lankester. "May I know what you are supposed to be?"

"You may not know. I don't know myself. Someone will tell me. But this you can bet your seat on—

your Westminster seat. When I return home in the small gray hours of tomorrow morning I shall have been either the success or the flop of the show. I've been sent down to talk to you. Bad luck, isn't it? How's the Prime Minister?"

"Very nicely, thank you."

"Good! And where's the next war going to break out?"

"Near East, I should say. Cheerful news for your father, anyway." .

Conrad frowned. War meant munitions, and munitions meant business, and business meant motor cars. Might even mean a motor car for himself, Conrad Shannon. A racer! But . . . oh, well, the world was a mad hat, anyway.

Conrad decided to talk about the weather. Instead he found himself saying:

"Look here, you don't mean it, do you?"

"What? War?" Lankester shrugged his shoulders. "Probably not. But who knows? War will go on till the world's temperature cools—and till every man can contemplate his own extinction."

Conrad stared at the speaker. This wasn't exactly ballroom talk! But it fascinated him. People didn't often trouble to talk to him seriously. Out of nowhere he shot the question:

"And till Father's munition factory goes bust?"

"No, munitions don't make war any more than peace conferences stop 'em. It's all a personal matter— and the moment you and I hear the drum, off we'll pop to the recruiting office." He laughed. "But meanwhile, Conrad, we are a Russian dancer and a golden cherub. Where's Dorothy?"

"Still adoring herself in her mirror," he answered, "but I admit she's got a case."

We have looked into two mirrors. A third gave back to its owner the face of Nell Gwynn framed in long, attractive ringlets. The ringlets fell almost to the gleaming shoulders, and the shoulders, hunched provocatively, escaped from a wide expanse of snowy lace.

Near by stood a man, watching. He was a very different proposition. His suit was practically a sheet of pearl buttons, and his coarse features needed no make-up to complete his conception of a coster king.

He had just arrived, and his small, narrow-set eyes, still smarting a little from the fog, were expressing definite approval.

"Like it?" inquired the woman, shifting her gaze from herself and regarding him through the mirror.

"Bloody all right," he answered.

"It's got to be," she observed, "or I stand to lose——"

She stopped abruptly.

"Go on, finish it," he urged. " 'Ow much do yer stand to lose, Sally?"

"Just as much, Sam, as I hope to make," she answered.

"And wot's that?"

"My business!"

"Oh, is it?" retorted Sam. "Then wot's *my* business?"

"To do what you're told, and to ask no questions," said Sally.

"Fer twenty quid," murmured Sam contemplatively.

"And damn good pay," declared Sally. "But for old times, Sam, I could have got plenty of others to do the job for half what I'm paying you!"

"Twenty quid," repeated Sam. "And 'ow much does that leave yer? Yus, 'ow much is somebody else payin' *you?*"

She did not answer. She was busy increasing the red of her lips.

"Muck!" commented Sam. "It on'y comes off and leaves a mark."

"Sometimes it's supposed to," smiled Sally.

Sam drew a step closer. No doubt about it, she was a stunner! Pity she'd gone up in the world and left him behind. She was a bit different now from the old days when they'd started working together. He was divided between resentment and admiration.

"It's a big risk fer twenty quid," he remarked, as she laid down the lipstick. "S'pose I don't think it's enough?"

"Making a bit of a nuisance of yourself, aren't you?" she responded.

"I said, s'pose I don't think it's enough?"

"Then you'll have to go on thinking, Sam."

"S'pose I do, and chuck the job."

"You wouldn't do that."

"You'd be dished if I did!"

"Don't you believe it!" But her heart stood still for a second. "I could get someone else."

"Not now, you couldn't."

She rounded on him, and her bright eyes flashed angrily.

"I could, and I would!" she exclaimed. "And to-morrow morning you'd wake up twenty pounds short— cursing yourself! Don't be a fool, boy! You're onto a good thing, and you hold onto it before it slips!"

"Gawd, you're a good looker!" muttered Sam. "Damn those toffs!"

The too-red lips curled deliberately. Sam discovered, to his secret mortification, that he was losing a little of his bravado. Her moving up in the world— that was what had done it. The same as him still, at heart, but working in higher circles.

"I wonder if I made a mistake," she said, quietly.

"Wot mistake?" he grunted.

"Trying to hand on a bit of my luck to an old pal? And a real, substantial slice, too."

"Well, Sally, we was pals once!"

"Am I forgetting it?"

"And I taught you some of your tricks. They was the fifty-fifty days. Now it's more like twenty to fifty, I shouldn't wunner!"

"So what are you going to do about it?" she inquired. "Quick, make up your mind."

Sam thought. He closed his eyes especially to do so. Then he made up his mind.

"This is wot I'm goin' to do about it, Sally," he said. "I won't stick you fer more than the twenty——"

"Good boy!"

"——but I'm goin' to stick you fer something else."

"Oh! Really?"

"Yus. Really!"

"Let's hear, then."

"You're goin' to 'ear, then! You're comin' back after the ball to this room—and I'm comin' back with yer! See?"

She sat very still. The notion appalled her. Sam was only half-correct in thinking that she had not changed in her heart. Crooked she remained, for crookedness had been ingrained in her before she had had any time to think about it. Ethically, her sins were as great as Sam's. But since she had escaped from the gutter which still held him she had acquired a certain fastidiousness, and physically her old pal was as repulsive to her now as once he had been attractive.

Yes, she had made a mistake. That rendered it all the more necessary not to make another. Controlling her repugnance, or the outward show of it—Sam could be ugly when he chose—she answered him.

"We'll see."

Sam shook his head.

"Not good enough," he said. "I want a promise."

"Even if I promised, would you believe me?"

"If a kiss went with it, I might," he grinned.

He took another step toward her chair. For an instant Sally saw red. Driven to it, she could be as ugly as Sam, but she had more control—that was one reason why she had risen out of the gutter and he had not—and she continued to sit very still while the murderous color came and went. Had she acted on her impulse to strike him, certain events at the Albert Hall a few hours later would have taken a very different course. When the instant had flown, she rose calmly from her dressing-table and advanced her lips toward his.

"You're a bad lad, Sam," she said, "but you're going to be a good lad afterward."

He took his prize. It was not quite as satisfactory

as he had hoped, for she pushed him away too soon, but it was enough to make him vow that he would secure bigger satisfaction later.

"Gawd, Sally, this is goin' to be a cinch for you!" he muttered thickly. "In that get-up you'd make jelly of the King o' Calcutta!"

"Let's hope you're right," she responded, returning to her dressing table and making up her lips again.

" 'Oo are you s'posed to be?"

"Ever heard of Nell Gwynn?"

"Wot, that tart?" He laughed. "Well, you know something about 'er game, don't yer?"

"How nicely put!"

"Oh, come off it! I expect that's why you chose the dress? Sort of 'ome from 'ome!"

"If you want the truth," she retorted, "I didn't choose it. It was chosen for me."

" 'Oo chose it?"

"A little bird. Well, let's be moving. Have you got your paraphernalia?"

"Me wot?"

"Sorry. I forgot you only knew words of one syllable. The things I asked you to bring?"

"Oh, *them,*" he replied, with a wink, and patted his bulging pockets. "But wot's the 'urry? It's a filthy night. Talk about pea soup! Let's stay 'ere fer a bit."

"I've got a job to do," she reminded him.

"Well, so've I, ain't I? But there's seven hours to do it in."

"I may need all that. Come on."

"Not even a drink?" he grumbled.

She relented. A drink was not a bad idea. She went to a little cupboard, and his eyes brightened as they followed her. A drop of something was what he wanted, to settle a nasty uncomfortable feeling that was gaining on him about the job.

"Let's 'ave a toast, Sally!" he cried, when she had brought the glasses.

"Right," she agreed. "What'll it be? The King?"

" 'Allo, wot's turned *you* patriotic all of a sudden?" he asked.

"Patriotic nothing!" she smiled. "The King I mean is Charles II."

With meticulous care, but an odd lack of enthusiasm, Warwick Hilling sat before a cracked looking-glass—our fourth and final mirror—completing his admirable transformation.

He was an admitted master in the art of make-up. He was, in fact, considerably better at making-up than he was at acting, which may have explained why he had spent most of his career abroad giving protean performances before All the Crowned Heads of the World. Before no Crowned Head, however, had he exhibited more skill than he was exhibiting at this moment, and his resemblance to the newspaper photograph, propped up against the mirror, on which he was modeling his features offered no possible scope for criticism.

The photograph had appeared that morning in a popular illustrated journal over the words, "Mr. Warwick Hilling, the Protean Actor, in the striking Balkan costume and make-up he will wear at the Chelsea Arts Ball tonight." But the photograph was not of Mr. Warwick Hilling. It had not even been sent to the illustrated journal by Mr. Warwick Hilling, or by his agent, or by anybody possessing his authority. It must have been sent, Hilling had decided, by the same mysterious hand that two days previously had sent him his instructions, accompanied by twenty-five one-pound notes and the promise of another twenty-five "to be paid, provided the said instructions are carried out, before 10:00 P.M. on the evening of December thirty-first, on completion of our business."

An actor whose chief attribute is his make-up, and who in these democratic days is mainly dependent on Crowned Heads for his audience, is liable to reach a time of life when twenty-five one-pound notes form a serious temptation. Warwick Hilling had reached that time. Penury had not destroyed his good looks and distinguished bearing. Everything about him—

even about the shiny suit now laid carefully aside on the plain, neat bed—proclaimed that once he had been successful, and that he was still a gentleman. But his success was now a fading memory, and even to keep a memory alive, one needs a minimum of warmth and food and creature-comfort.

So Hilling had kept the notes. There was indeed no address to which they could have been returned. And when in response to a mysterious telephone call he had confirmed his acceptance, he had faithfully attended to the instructions.

The instructions were odd, but simple. He was to make it known that he was going to the Chelsea Arts Ball. He was to buy the ticket personally and he was to talk freely and loudly about it, declaring that he would wear the costume of one of the Crowned Heads before whom he had performed. In order to complete the illusion he would even remain silent throughout the evening, lest his accent should mar the effect; and, although he could not recall having granted an interview to any reporter, his intention was duly published in the press.

The costume itself had turned up, anonymously, that morning. The parcel containing it, together with the original of his alleged newspaper photograph, appeared with his breakfast tray. And in the parcel was a further note, bearing further instructions:

"The writer has had occasion to learn of your skill at face-transformation and impersonation, and is therefore confident that you will have no difficulty in copying the features of the picture you will find, with your name under it, in today's daily press. In case of accidents, however, an original copy of the photograph is included herewith. Also in case of accidents, you are requested to burn this letter as soon as you have read it, and to continue to conduct the whole matter with the utmost secrecy and discretion. At 9:00 P.M. you will be ready, dressed and transformed. Between that hour and 10:00 P.M. you will be visited, and you will receive the final half of your fee. Till then!"

So here Warwick Hilling sat, as the clock ticked away anxious minutes on the last day of the year, in the perfect guise of a Balkan Prince, awaiting the next step with outward calm but inward trepidation.

"Of course, all this is splendid publicity for me," he reflected, endeavoring in these moments of trying tension to keep his mind busy and cheerful, "and it may even put me back on the map." Only in his private thoughts did he admit that he was no longer on the map. "If I can keep near the press photographers I might get my photograph in the papers a second time—yes, genuinely, the second time—and

then that damned agent may begin to take an interest
in me again. Even the No. 2 towns. . . . And meanwhile, whatever happens," he added, forcing his mind
away from the rather depressing contemplation of the
No. 2 towns, "I have £17 6s. 3d. in my pocket, with
another £25—plus an excellent supper—to come!"

He had fasted religiously since morning in the prospect of this excellent supper to come. Fasting in these
lean days was an art in which he was well practiced.

"Yes, but what, in the name of the Immortal Bard,
is it all *about?*" he exclaimed, suddenly resuming
his cogitations after a period of mental blankness.
"Really—this seems incredible!"

Outside his window curled the cloak of fog. Fog
was everywhere, physically and mentally. All at once
he shivered. He imagined he heard somebody knocking on the door. He became annoyed with himself.
"Though, true," he reflected, "all real artists have
nerves." Then he jumped up from his chair. Somebody *was* knocking!

He jerked his head round quickly. The action was
peculiarly inappropriate to his dignified role. Yet
perhaps a Balkan Prince could be swift as well as
imposing, with a heart that beat tumultuously beneath
a passive exterior? A voice sounded from the landing.
His landlady's voice. Until two days ago her voice

had rankled, but it had taken a turn for the better since she had received somewhat unexpectedly her rent.

"The chauffeur, sir," she called. "Your car's here."

Chauffeur? Car?

Then the door opened, and the chauffeur entered. He was a short man, almost squat, and the landlady behind him could easily feast her eyes over the top of his head at the splendid vision of Mr. Hilling. But only for a moment was the vision permitted to her inferior eyes. The chauffeur abruptly closed the door, shutting her out.

For a few moments the two men regarded each other in silence, while the disgruntled landlady, cheated of a full-length memory, shuffled downstairs. The chauffeur was composed. Hilling merely appeared so. A queer chill had entered the room with the chauffeur, a chill that was more disconcerting than the fog. Fog was British. . . .

The chauffeur's opening words, however, were satisfactory.

"Good! So! Good!" he said.

He spoke with an accent, but with the assurance of one for whom language had no terrors.

"I am glad you approve," answered Hilling, rather stiffly. "You are—er—driving me to the Hall?"

"In a minute I drive—to the Hall, yes," nodded the

chauffeur, his bright, very live eyes still boring. Hilling noticed the little pause that broke up the statement. "Yes, in a minute. But, first, some questions. All is done as you are instructed?"

"You observe," retorted Hilling, holding out his arms impressively. He did not quite like that word "instructed." It savored too much of a master speaking to a servant, and the only master Hilling acknowledged, as he had boasted on countless occasions, was his art.

"Good, so!" smiled the little chauffeur. "I observe! But I observe only that which I see. All has been done with discretion?"

"Naturally, sir!"

"Good, naturally. You have said only what was to be said? No more? You burn the letter?" The chauffeur waited till Hilling nodded. "And you have bought the ticket for the ball, good, naturally?"

"I understood that was a part of the contract."

"To mean that you have bought it, that is so?"

"I have bought it."

"Show me, pray."

Hilling waved toward the mantelpiece on which the ticket reigned among lesser objects.

"Ah!" murmured the chauffeur, and speeding to the mantelpiece he took the ticket and pocketed it.

Hilling frowned.

"I shall need the ticket, to get in," he reminded his visitor.

"But if you do not get in, you do not need the ticket," answered the chauffeur briskly.

"I beg your pardon?" exclaimed Hilling, astonished.

"I explain," replied the chauffeur. "But, no, first I show you the good faith. That is the English way, good, so?" He produced a bundle of notes as he spoke and laid them on the table. "You expect twenty-five. Observe there are twenty-six one-pound and one ten-shilling, and now I add a one-shilling piece and a six-pence piece." He did so. "So we have the twenty-five we arrange, with also the cost of the ticket, good, so?" He smiled amiably. "There is no charge for the costume."

"I—I am afraid, sir, I do not understand you," murmured Hilling, restraining an impulse to snatch the notes lest they, like the ticket, should vanish. "Do I not go to the ball?"

"No. I explain," repeated the chauffeur, still smiling amiably. "It is so. You go down the stairs with me to the car. So many stairs! They make one to puff! But no matter. You have order the car, make remember of that. In the hall is the landlady of the house. Oh, yes, I know the English landlady. She is— you have a strange word for it—ah, agog. She is agog. She sees us get in. Good, so! You in front of me, make note. But as you open the door I step back and tread on her toe, and while she cries 'Ah!' you are in the car, and the door is quick closed, so she does not see another in the car because I tread onto her toe and it is dark and he sit well back and it is a fog. But, pah!" He waved his little fat hands contemptuously. "We do not need your fog. We arrange it all, what is your word, ah, in the water-tight. Then, voilà, off we go!"

"Voilà? You are French?" asked Hilling, catching at straws.

The chauffeur laughed amusedly. "No! Voilà, it is all the world over. Japan, even."

"Where do we go off to?" inquired Hilling, fighting against a sensation that he was in a dream, and not necessarily a good dream.

"To your Albert Hall," returned the chauffeur. "Me, I drive there."

"But I understood you to say——"

"That you do not go to the ball? So! You do not go to the ball. It is the other man who will go to the ball, the other man who sit well back, but who get out at your Albert Hall, yes, the other man so like you, and you so like him, eh? The brain, it clears?"

"I—see," muttered Hilling slowly. "Yes—I see. The man whose photograph——"

"Was in the papers. I send it. And the interview.

I send it. I arrange it. For me, the work. For you——" He snapped his fingers toward the notes. "And now come, it is the time."

But Hilling paused. His head was spinning. There was something likable about the chauffeur, but the sensation that the dream was not a good dream increased each moment. It might be risky to inquire further; inquiry might eliminate the chauffeur's likable quality, and substitute one less appealing. Those bright, live eyes might not be pleasant to encounter in another mood. Still, would the conscience of Warwick Hilling remain passive if its owner funked the risk? Hilling was a bad actor, but he was not a bad man, and the two, despite the critics, can be separate.

"One moment, sir," said Hilling, as his visitor made for the door.

"There is no moment," answered the chauffeur, without stopping.

"I insist!"

"So? Insist?" Now the chauffeur stopped, and for an instant anger dawned in his eyes. But he drove the anger away with a quick shrug, and waited.

Three questions raced round Hilling's mind. Two were easy to ask, the third was not. He began with the simplest and most obvious.

"What happens to me, when the other man gets out of the car at the Albert Hall?"

"We drive away," replied the chauffeur simply. "And—presently—I drive you back." He added, reassuringly, "I look after you. You are all right."

It was not a very satisfactory response, but Hilling passed on to the next.

"How did you come to select me for this—business?" was the second question.

"You ask much!"

"In another sense, sir, I could quote that back."

It pleased Hilling to find that he was keeping up his end with fair credit. Occasionally, on the stage, he had been forced to deal with unruly members of second-rate audiences (for all his audiences were not composed of Crowned Heads) who did not understand serious Art, and his somewhat massive repartee rarely failed.

"Well, perhaps it hurts nothing that you know," said the chauffeur. "You have performed in Europe? Before, as you say in the announcement, the Crowned Heads, so? In one place, then, you were remembered. And when I am here, in your country, I am here to keep the eyes open. So I know of your great talent, Mr. Hilling, and I know also, if you pardon me, of your—difficulties?" He glanced expressively round the shabby room. "And now I hope there is no more question?"

"Just one, I am afraid, sir."

"Then, quick!"

"It is more quickly asked than answered, perhaps. If I am to know little, this I must know. I have my code, and my pride. Yes, sir, even though I also have, as you have just remarked, my difficulties. This—this role of mine—is it a role I shall play with—honor?"

The rather theatrical dignity with which this speech was delivered had a surprising effect upon the little chauffeur. At the words "code" and "pride" a new light sprang into his eye, and he stiffened slightly. Then he stood silent for several seconds, considering.

"Sir," he said at last, in a tone hardly less theatrical than Hilling's, "let the mind be at peace. The world, it is strange. We poor people, what do we know? In God only lies all knowledge. But the part you play is honorable!" He thumped his chest tremendously. "Good, so?"

He held out his hand. Hilling took it, satisfied. But he descended the stairs with his head in a whirl.

TEN P.M.

HENRY BROWN had never been in a taxi before, and
it was unfortunate for him that his initiation should
occur in a fog. He had looked forward to the ride
with exaggerated keenness. He had anticipated a journey of nippy speed, of cutting round corners, of passing things; instead, the taxi crawled at pedestrian pace,
cheating him of the mildest thrill and giving him
more time than he desired for thought. He did not
want to think. Thought showed one up! He wanted
to plunge rapidly into his adventure, to be caught up
quickly into the current that would carry him into
the center of it. He wanted to find himself lost in a
maze of light and color and movement in which there
was no responsibility, and from which there was no
escape. But here he was, creeping forward at a snail's
gait, stopping, going on again, stopping, going on
again, stopping. And every time the taxi stopped he
was given the opportunity to put his head out the window and instruct the driver to return.

He had even been unlucky in his taxi. It was old

and worn, with a cracked window and a hard seat. "Why don't they let us choose?" he grumbled. The next one on the rank had been a beauty. One of the newest type, with curved glass windows. He would have been quite happy in that. But apparently there was no question of personal choice. When he had mumbled his preference, he had nearly had his head bitten off! And then, after nearly having his head bitten off, the driver of the taxi that was forced upon him had winked at him. He was quite sure the driver of the superior taxi would not have done that. The driver of the superior taxi had been a superior man, with shiny black leggings and a smart cloth cap. His own driver was as old and as worn as his cab, and he sat on his seat sideways, with hunched shoulders. No style whatever about the fellow! Worse still, he called out rude remarks to other drivers, and was once reprimanded for something by a policeman. It was foul luck.

But presently, as they progressed westward through the fog, new sensations began to percolate through Henry, changing his mood. He forgot the cab, and concentrated on himself. Sometimes the sensations were pleasant, sometimes they were not. In confusing succession he passed from tingling excitement to warm delight, from warm delight to chilly fear, from chilly fear to nausea. The nausea alarmed him. At one ter-

rible moment, when the taxi stopped with a sharp jolt
and he thought he had arrived, he really believed he
was going to be sick. But he controlled himself with
a herculean effort, the danger passed, and the taxi
lurched on again.

"Now, look here," he admonished himself, very
earnestly, "this won't *do!*"

Through smeared windows he watched great clus-
ters of lights that looked like approaching night cities
and materialized into ordinary motorbusses. Lamp
posts grew out of nothing, and vanished back into
nothing. Now he was alone in a great dark region.
Now he was surrounded by sudden illumination. A
car at right-angles abruptly blocked their way. "Whew,
that's had a skid!" he thought. It appeared to be aim-
ing straight for a wall. A moment later it moved on
without turning, and apparently glided right through
the wall.

"That's funny!" thought Henry. "Am I wonky?"

The question was answered when his taxi began
moving backward. Actually it was not moving at all,
but the next taxi was moving forward. A very posh
car glided up, taking the place of the taxi that had
moved on ahead. It stopped beside his. A face appeared at the window. A girl's face. "Whew!" muttered Henry. "She's staring right in!" He pressed
himself back in his corner. He hoped his beret was

lost among the shadows. She smiled. The smile sent a pang through his heart. Whew!

Then the face disappeared, and another was substituted. Henry did not believe his eyes. It was a gold face. "Here, don't be silly!" he thought, startled. The gold face almost frightened him, and he closed his eyes. When he opened them the gold face was gone and his taxi was moving again.

He decided not to remember the gold face. It hadn't been nice. He remembered instead the girl's face. That *had* been nice. And the girl's face, moreover, had been real. Was it going to the ball? Yes, it must be going to the ball, for now everything seemed to be going to the ball, and there was a sense as of a slow current sucking all the vehicles in one direction. He no longer felt lonely. A face he knew would be there. He would search for it, if he had to search all night. For the entire seven hours. (He knew it was seven hours, because he had worked out ,the cost per hour and it was exactly four and six, or just under a penny a minute.) He was bad at remembering faces, and frequently recognized the wrong people or failed to recognize the right, and he had already forgotten exactly what this girl's face was like; but he was sure he would recognize it when he saw it again, and the conviction brought him a strange warmth and happiness.

Hallo! Things were happening! His taxi had entered a sort of covered way, and it had stopped again, and the driver was gesticulating at him through the window. "Move along, there!" cried a policeman. In a panic Henry opened the door and leaped out. "Where do I go?" he asked the person he leaped into. It was one of the countless touts who haunt the outside of the Albert Hall on big occasions, trying to pick up easily-earned sixpences.

"Foller me, sir," replied the tout. He spoke with a hectoring, semiofficial air, exuding the impression that Henry would be imprisoned if he were disobedient. "White ticket? This way."

He seized Henry's arm, lest Henry should escape and part with sixpence to somebody else.

"Hi! Where's my fare?" bawled the taximan.

"Move along, there!" cried the policeman.

Henry wrenched his arm free and turned back to the cab.

"Thought you were goin' to get away with it!" grinned the taximan good-naturedly.

But in his super-sensitive condition Henry mistook the good-nature for sarcasm, and he replied, in a shrill squeak:

"What do you mean; do you suppose I'd play a dirty trick like that on a person?"

The too-heated defense lacked the intended dignity.

People turned their heads and smiled. He cursed himself. Why had he spoken so loudly? To prove that he did not mind he spoke more loudly still. "What's the fare?" he cried.

"Three-and-six," answered the taximan. "On the clock."

The addition meant that three-and-six on a clock did not mean three-and-six to a gentleman. Henry thrust two half crowns at him and hurried away, aghast at himself. He no longer thought of his voice. He thought of those two half crowns. Five bob! That made a hole! But he had to get away, and to start afresh. Fortunately the Albert Hall was a large place, and perhaps he would never meet any of these people again. And others would not know.

The tout was still at his elbow. He had sized the incident up, and he stuck like a leech. Henry found his arm seized once more.

"This way, you foller me," said the tout.

Henry did not like the look of the fellow. By comparison, the taximan was almost lovable. Why *should* he follow him? In spite of the tout's disturbingly insistent manner Henry was convinced that he was not actually an official or anything. If a small cinema could afford uniforms, it was obvious the Albert Hall could!

"Come *on!*" barked the tout, as Henry hesitated.

"Yes, but wait a moment," murmured Henry.

"What for—you wanter git in, doncher?" retorted the tout, his tone suggesting that to get in was going to be terribly difficult. "White ticket, that's the main entrance, come on." And then he made a psychological mistake that cost him his sixpence. "Do as I tell yer!" he threatened.

Up to a point he had read Henry correctly. Henry was a weak man; a weak man who was confused, wavering, self-conscious. He would dread a scene. But Henry was also in that sensitive condition that may carry even a weak man into a temporary semblance of strength. He had made a bad start when he had got out of the taxi. He was not going to confirm this horrible sense of inferiority by a second bad move now. The group of people who had witnessed his first disgrace and whom he devoutly hoped he would never encounter again had flowed away from him, and he was now in the middle of another quite different group. If he allowed himself to be hectored before these new people, also, the number of potential plague spots within the hall itself would be doubled! But, quite apart from them, Henry Brown had to get right with himself.

He stopped walking. The tout had been pulling him along. Two massive men behind him nearly strode into his back, separated abruptly like a large divided germ, sprayed round him, and joined again beyond. *They* weren't being led by anybody!

"Now, then, you listen to me," said Henry, in a voice surprisingly firm. "I don't want you, see? You're not going to get anything out of me, not a thing. Go away at once, this minute, or I'll call a policeman. See?"

Then he walked on again, and to his relief the tout fell behind. But the disappointed guide called after him. He called him a bloody little something. Henry reached the main entrance scarlet but triumphant.

He joined a little swirl and was carried by it up some wide steps to an open glass door. An official—a genuine official this time—took his ticket. "Oh—you take the whole of it?" jerked Henry. The official did not answer, being busy taking the whole of somebody else's ticket. Henry hoped it was all right. With the complete ticket gone he now had nothing to show that he was entitled to supper. Perhaps you got a special ticket for supper inside. He would have to keep his eyes open. He must be careful not to ask silly questions. Very likely he would see a sign somewhere saying: "Supper Tickets."

Strangely-dressed human beings were ahead of him. Others, behind, pressed him forward into a large vestibule. Some of the costumes were fully displayed, some gleamed from beneath expensive overcoats. Sud-

denly Henry got in a panic about his own overcoat.
It was worn and shiny, and half an hour's steady
brushing had increased the shine. He must get rid
of it as soon as he could. He supposed there was a
cloakroom somewhere about. He spotted the two massive men who had nearly barged into his back. He
followed them. He went down a wide, curved staircase. A girl, coming up the stairs, smiled at him.

"My God!" thought Henry, and stopped as abruptly
as though he had been shot.

For this was not a derisive smile. It was a friendly
smile. He could not quite believe it. He multiplied
its importance by one million. Perhaps he did not
look so horrible, after all? Here, among all these
others? Perhaps he would "pass." Warmth surged
through him, followed by sharp despair. He had not
smiled back!

He turned. She was out of sight. "Damn!" he
muttered.

He continued down the stairs, and caught up with
the two massive gentlemen as they were handing their
coats across a counter. They were now wonderful red
generals. There was a saucer on the counter, its pattern
obscured by silver coins. No copper ones. Pity. He
watched the generals to see how much they put in.
Sixpence each. He felt relieved. Now *he* need not
put in more than sixpence. "Program, sir?" inquired

a voice in his ear. "Eh? No," he answered, from force of habit. He hardly ever bought programs; you could nearly always snip an announcement or advertisement out of a paper, or get a squint at somebody else's program. But the program seller paid no attention to his negative, thrust a program into his hand, and demanded a shilling. "Of course, he's right; I don't know what I was thinking about," reflected Henry, hypnotized into becoming worth a shilling less. A shilling, to Henry, was a complete lunch. "Naturally, one needs a program." Now the man behind the counter was taking *his* overcoat. The two red generals were standing by, lighting cigarettes. Henry felt in his trouser pocket. Oh, of course, he hadn't got any trouser pockets. He groped in his wide velvet-jacket pockets. All the money he had in the world was in his overcoat and his shoes.

He asked for his overcoat back. He received it back, while somebody behind him commented, "This chap's in for an all-night job." He rescued three silver pieces, two florins and one half crown. Nothing smaller. "Whew!" he thought. "Can one take change?" If one could, it needed more courage than Henry possessed with people pressing against his back. He threw the half crown into the saucer. He had meant to throw in one of the florins, but had missed.

"Your ticket, sir," said the man behind the counter, without even thanking him.

He took the ticket mechanically, and mechanically noticed that the number was 789. Then, with fingers itching and finance tottering, he turned away. He did not remember till long afterward that he had left his program on the counter.

He took out a cigarette, to steady himself. One of the red generals paused in the operation of blowing out his match and offered it. Henry immediately felt better. It almost made him wish he'd entered the army. "Thenks," he said, as he accepted the light. "Thenks."

It was bewildering. Hell one moment, and heaven the next! Which would win? The world was topsy-turvy! Would everybody accept him like this? Red generals, girls on stairs, everybody? For the entire seven hours that stretched ahead of him like a magnificently impossible adventure? This was worth four-and-six an hour, this was! No matter what happened. He'd come every year. He'd even cut his summer holiday short, if necessary. To think that this had been going on regularly, year after year, and he had never realized it!

He searched for a looking-glass before ascending the stairs. He found one in a lavatory. He regarded himself. That was a mistake. But he reflected as he walked hastily away that one couldn't really judge one's own face, could one? He knew he had read that somewhere. If he had looked to those red generals as he looked to himself, he would never have been offered that light!

He returned to the staircase. He joined a little throng that bore him upward. As he passed the spot where the girl had smiled at him—he had now entirely forgotten the girl who had smiled at him from the posh car—he stared at it. It held a little thrilling memory. But many bigger thrills lay ahead of Henry Brown.

Now he was at the top of the staircase. Now he was crossing a big space. Now he was in a wide curving corridor. There were doors in the curved inner walls. Most of the doors were closed, but some were ajar, and a few were open, yielding tantalizing glimpses of neat private boxes with elegant chairs and tables and flowers. At regular intervals the curved walls were interrupted by passages. He drifted into one of the passages. On each side of the passage, standing like a sentinel, was a tall beef-eater. He walked between them. He stopped dead, and caught his breath.

Before him was the ballroom. Unbelievably vast, unbelievably dazzling, unbelievably colorful. He found himself in an entirely new world, a world of blatant joy and garish, almost frightening fascination. In the distance, beyond the moving forms of uncountable dancers, was a great orchestra, and beyond the orchestra were, surely, the golden clouds of heaven itself. He had never seen such gold. He had never pictured such immensity. And balloons—thousands of balloons, festooning down from the dizzy ceiling like bunches of enormous, many-colored grapes. . . .

Things he did not know of stirred within him.

"Enjoying it?" asked Harold Lankester, as he danced by with Dorothy Shannon.

"Lovely!" she answered. "Are you?"

"Of course," he replied. "But isn't the whole thing mad?"

"Then why did you come?"

"Because I'm as mad as the rest. Or perhaps to escape from another form of madness. I've been talking politics all the afternoon, and I'm supposed to be at a political conference tonight."

"Sorry I'm keeping you from your duty, Massine! Or are you Idzikowski?"

He smiled.

"*You* kept quite a number of people from their duty, Madame du Barry," he said. "Even political duty."

"Oh, let's switch off politics," she sighed. "Father's been going potty with them lately. What do you think

of his costume? Between you and me, I fancy he
rather likes himself! And Conrad—there he is, with
Mother, bumping into that girl undressed as a Hawai-
ian Venus. I say, some of the dresses are rather absent, aren't they? What do you think of Conrad?"

"Unique."

"Let's hope he is! But don't you think Mother's
rather sweet?"

"She's delightful."

"Tell her so. It'll please her. Oh, look!" she exclaimed suddenly. "Isn't he *wonderful!*"

Lankester turned his head and followed the direction of her eyes. They were resting on an imposing
figure standing in one of the entrances to the dancing
floor. It was the figure of a Balkan Prince. He had
just arrived, alone. Near him stood a less impressive
figure wearing a velvet jacket, loud check slacks, and
an enormous beret.

"By Jove!" murmured Lankester, no less interested.

"You'd think it was the real thing," said Dorothy,
"but, of course, it's not. It's some actor or other.
Oh, and look at that funny little fellow almost beside
him. I saw him from our car on our way here."

Then they flowed on in the roundabout.

The man who ought to have told Mrs. Shannon that
she looked delightful, but who had failed to do so, sat
by himself in Box 12, watching.

Mr. Shannon was glad to be alone in the box. He hoped, little realizing what lay ahead of him, that he would be alone most of the evening. That was why when the girl who was to have been the sixth member of their party had suddenly contracted measles he had discouraged any eleventh-hour attempt to secure a substitute. Now Conrad would have to dance with his mother, and Mr. Shannon himself would be released. This might be bad luck on Conrad. Mr. Shannon was rather depressingly aware that youth calls to youth. But since Conrad was young he had plenty of flings ahead of him, and tonight Mr. Shannon wanted a fling of the only kind he himself had left—a fling into the glorious orgies of audacious imagination.

He was fond of his wife, but he could dance with her any night he chose to the radio or the gramophone. Much pleasanter now, he decided as he sat well forward in his box, to be alone so that he could imagine himself partnering these other women with their unknown bodies and tempting skins—to imagine, in fact, that he actually *was* Charles II, possessing the royal prerogative to smile at whom he willed, to dance with whom he willed, and to take home whom he willed. He had the list of Charles's paramours by heart. Lucy Walter, "beautiful, bold, but insipid"; Catherine Pegg; the magnificent Lady Castlemaine;

Mrs. Stewart; and above all, and most famous of all, provocative Nell Gwynn, Sweet Nell of Old Drury. . . .

As Mr. Shannon's mind dwelt on a picture he had recently studied of Nell Gwynn with more than esthetic interest, he smiled dreamily and vapidly from his box; and when Nell Gwynn smiled back at him, he thought at first that he was the victim of some pretty trick of fancy. Enjoying the trick, and in no hurry to end so charming an illusion, he augmented his smile . . . and then suddenly discovered that this was no fancy, and that Nell Gwynn was actually smiling at him from the outskirts of the dancing floor.

His heart jumped. He felt like a caught criminal. But even while his forehead became damp, he found a fearful delight in his criminality, and for a fatal instant—for the instant that is one instant too long— he hung onto the smile, praying that no one apart from Nell saw him, and that his wife was at the farthest end of the hall.

That should have been the end of it. As matters eventually transpired, it was only the merest beginning of it. The materialized vision of seventeenth-century loveliness stopped outside his box. She appeared to have dropped something, and her partner, a coster in a marvelous costume of pearl buttons, stooped at her murmured command to regain it. In that moment Charles II, alias Mr. James Shannon, received a very definite wink.

Then the pearly king rose with a fan, and the couple danced away.

"You look hot, my dear," observed a placid voice behind him.

Mrs. Shannon had returned, with her gilded son in tow.

"Do I, dear?" answered Mr. Shannon carefully. He wiped his forehead with his lace handkerchief. "So I am. These wigs are like ovens."

"If you sat in the back of the box, you could take it off," suggested Mrs. Shannon.

"Gold, too, hath its heat," murmured Conrad. "I think next year I shall be a sun-bather. Or Gandhi. 'Strewth, that's a brain wave! Gandhi!"

"Then you won't be dancing next year with your old mother," retorted Mrs. Shannon. Turning back to her husband, she added, "Have you *seen* that sun-bathing couple, Jim? I know we're modern and all that, but personally I call it disgraceful!"

"Eh? No," answered Mr. Shannon. Actually he had seen them, and when they had passed his box his eyes had nearly left their sockets to follow them. "Disgraceful, are they? I wonder it's allowed."

"Hush, not before the children!" whispered Conrad, as Dorothy and Lankester entered

The music had stopped. A queer, momentary heaviness hung in the air. The figure of the Balkan Prince strolled slowly by, with easy grace.

"Aren't we all silent?" said Conrad.

They all began talking.

"Well, *you* 'aven't lost no time," grinned Sam.

"I haven't got any time to lose," replied Sally.

"Bah, you can 'ook 'im before midnight," retorted Sam. "The perishin' sop!"

They were sitting on one of the sofas in the outer corridor. They had it to themselves. Later, the sofas would fill up, when the dancing had lost its glamour and couples preferred to sit and whisper, but now the outer corridor was comparatively deserted.

"You don't think much of him?" inquired Sally.

"Think much of 'im? I don't think nothing of 'im," said Sam. "If that simperin' old fool is like King Charles II, they make 'em better now!"

"Just the same, he's not a fool—excepting in the way I'm going to make him one."

"That's right, Sall! It's all You with a capital letter! Leave *me* out of it!"

"He's boss of a pretty big business."

"Oh? And wot's the business?"

"Munitions."

"Wot, bombs?"

"I expect so. That sort of thing, anyway."

Sam whistled softly. Without moving his head he moved his eyes, and looked at her out of the corner of them.

"Onto real big stuff, eh?"

"Well, it's not small stuff."

"Corse, it'd be a pity to *tell* me anything, wouldn't it?"

"The less you know, the sounder you'll sleep."

"Gawd, think I'm a suckling!" he muttered disgustedly. "Yus, and 'oo taught yer that, anyway?"

"You did, Sam. See what a good pupil I am?"

"Good pupil be blowed! Where's the *gratitood?*"

"You'll have twenty pounds worth of gratitude in your pocket tomorrow, if you're a good boy," she reminded him.

"I'll 'ave a bit more than that by tomorrow, don't *you* worry!" he reminded her back. "You make the rest of 'em 'ere look sick!"

Now he turned his head, and looked at her directly. She smiled back coolly, but she was thinking, "I'll have to find some way of getting rid of him when we're through."

"So it's them bombs, is it?" said Sam, after a little pause. "I 'ope 'e ain't got one in 'is little pocket!"

"Well, you've got something in *your* little pocket," answered Sally.

"That's right, so I 'ave," he grinned. *"I'll* bomb 'im!" Then suddenly the grin vanished, and he looked dark. "Yus, and if 'e gets fresh with you, I'll give 'im something else 'e won't ferget!"

He spoke with feeling. With equal feeling Sally retorted:

"What's the matter with you? Are you going daft? He's got to get fresh, hasn't he?"

Sam glowered.

"Now, listen, Sam," she went on, and her voice grew hard. "There's to be no nonsense, do you hear? You'll do your job, neither more nor less, and if that's not clear, you can quit right now!"

Sam did not respond for a few seconds. Then he shrugged his shoulders. "I'll do my job, don't worry," he said. "And get full payment for it. If you think——"

He paused. Someone was passing slowly. He waited.

" 'Oo was that?" he muttered, when the figure had strolled leisurely by. "The blinkin' Prince o' Roorey-tania?"

"Oh, come along!" snapped Sally, jumping up nervously. "Let's have a drink!"

Warwick Hilling sat alone inside a saloon car as it drove away from the Albert Hall, and he pondered.

"I have been through many interesting experiences in my life," he thought. "I have acted before Foreign Kings and I have been the hind legs of a horse." (Only he and the front legs of the horse had ever known that he had been the hind legs of the horse.) "I have been in an airplane crash. I have traveled first-class with a bus ticket. I have—I regret—known Mademoiselle from Armentieres. On the other hand," came a swift whitewashing reflection, "I have refused a greater gift from a good woman. I have stuck a bayonet into the chest of a fellow-creature—'Foul-drugged with Duty, I have watched his pain, and with a shudd'ring laugh have thrust again.'" He reviewed these ghosts of the past with dispassionate interest, seeing himself as a player of parts. Then, swinging back to the present as the saloon car slid round a corner, he concluded, "But have I ever—I ask, I do not state—have I ever encountered an incident which, for unusualness, transcends—this?"

Hilling usually thought in actual words. He believed in clear enunciation of the mind as well as of the tongue, and he found that, in thought, his words were invariably effective. But now he leaned back against the immense comfort of well-sprung cushions and reviewed, not in words, but in a series of pictures, the events of the last half hour.

The little chauffeur, whose back Hilling could see

as a dark smudge pressed against the dividing glass, had been correct in his forecast. The landlady had been waiting in the front hall, pretending unnecessarily that she was merely putting pictures straight. "Dear me, these picture frames!" she had even murmured as Hilling and the chauffeur had descended the stairs. " 'Ow they get shook about beats me!" She had sprung to the door to open it. She had simpered with appreciative respect as Hilling, who really looked impressive, strode by her wordlessly and descended the cracking stone steps to the street. Her eyes had remained glued on him while he descended, while he reached the splendid car, while he paused for an instant, and while he opened the polished door. And then, suddenly, she had started, wincing at an abrupt pain in her foot.

"But pardon!" cried the chauffeur's voice in her ear.

She had turned angrily to meet the smiling apology of the careless fellow who had trodden on her foot. He had not looked very contrite, but her just anger was quelled by the very quality of his composure. There was something in it that froze her.

"I make to pass, Madame. Permit me, yes?"

She had stood aside. He had passed out onto the cracking stone stairs. Then, suddenly realizing that this annoying man was cheating her a second time, she had clapped her eyes again upon the car.. Too late! Her lodger, who a week ago had been anathema but who was now healing balm, was in the car, and was to be seen no more.

The chauffeur took his seat at the wheel, and the car glided off.

Inside the saloon was darkness. The little glass globe set snugly in the roof gave no light. It showed dimly, palely, like the ghost of itself. Something else showed dimly and palely, also, in the farthest corner. Hilling knew it was a face. A face resembling his, and therefore even more like a ghost. But he did not look at it. He had an idea he was not supposed to, and he certainly did not want to. It merely came for a brief instant into the range of a corner of his eye. Yes, it was unpleasantly like a ghost, completely shrouded saving for the face. Hilling fought a nasty sensation that he was dead.

The fog outside the window assisted the disturbing illusion giving him a suffocating feeling. It was like thick yellow earth.

The journey through the fog was silent; stiflingly monotonous. Hilling's ghost did not break it, and so he assumed he was right not to break it himself. He had read every book on regal etiquette and he knew that conversation was royalty's prerogative. Speak when a king speaks to you. The same with a prince.

A Balkan Prince, anyway. Not necessarily an English Prince. English Princes sometimes fraternized. Good chaps, English Princes. . . .

The slow and painful journey was broken by only one incident. It was an incident that suggested a Balkan Prince could fraternize, also, if he wanted to. But suddenly, unconversationally. All at once Hilling became conscious of something small and white and thin before his nose. A cigarette!

It appeared to be suspended in mid-air, and thus carried on the ghostly attributes of everything inside that car. He did not know that, a few seconds previously, an entire case of cigarettes had been held before his glazed, unseeing eyes, and that the single cigarette had subsequently been extracted by the donor as, possibly, a more effective way of attracting his attention. His fingers rose to the cigarette convulsively. At least, he supposed they were his fingers, but they seemed to have been attracted up to the cigarette by a will not his own. They touched the cigarette and held it. Then a small light glowed before his face. It glowed above a little gold lighter. Mechanically he put the cigarette between his lips and lit it. The light vanished. Ahead of him now was a wisp of curling, gray-blue smoke.

Even if the cigarette had been drugged he would have puffed it. But only Hilling's mind was drugged. Drugged with the strangeness of the occasion.

That had been all, until at last the car had completed its journey and had stopped at its destination.

The sense that everything had been planned and worked out to its final detail was increased by the fact that, when the car stopped, Hilling found himself in the corner farthest from the pavement. He was convinced that this was not accidental. He did not have to move, or to show himself. He was as secure from eyes in his corner as, when he had entered the car, the Balkan Prince had been in his. The Balkan Prince slipped out of the car. The door closed. The next instant the car moved on again. Now Warwick Hilling was alone with his thoughts. . . .

"And what happens next?" he wondered, after he had relived all these incidents in his mind, and the great hall in which he was supposed to be had been blotted out behind him by the fog. "Am I driven home? Or what?"

A study of the geographical position suggested that he was not being driven home, although it was not easy to study geography through the yellow haze. Home lay east, and the car appeared to be traveling west. Not straight west. Zigzag west. Why west? And, even more interesting, why zigzag?

"We might be trying to shake off a snake!" reflected Hilling.

The reflection put a startling idea into his head. Perhaps they were!

Now left, now right, now straight for a block, now left. And, surely, at an unnecessary speed? Too fast for a fog? He bent close to the window and peered out. A panel of the glass dividing him from the chauffeur slid aside, and the chauffeur's voice came through.

"Not that!" called the chauffeur.

His voice was quiet, but authoritative.

"Why not?" demanded Hilling.

"And ask no question," answered the chauffeur. "Please to sit back."

Hilling obeyed, but he felt a little ruffled. His own voice had annoyed him as much as the chauffeur's. Because it was so long since he had used it, it had been thick and unimposing. He cleared his throat softly, then inquired with dignity:

"Am I not to know where we are going?"

"You know sometime," came the retort.

"You are too kind!" murmured Hilling.

"Good, so!" smiled the chauffeur.

Hilling saw the smile in the windscreen, and realized then how the chauffeur had seen him at the window.

"I hope it will prove good, so!" observed Hilling, after a little pause. "You must admit I am patient."

"Like, as you say, the monument."

"And trusting."

"To trust, it is good when you can."

"There, sir, I am with you," replied Hilling, and cleared his throat again softly to add, " 'Shed without shame each virtue, an you must, If it shall leave inviolate your trust.' But sometimes one's trust is put to a severe strain. And this, undoubtedly, is one of those times."

"To talk and to drive together, it is forbid," answered the chauffeur. "So, the accident."

He slid the glass panel to as he spoke. But Hilling was not in a mood to be dismissed in this peremptory fashion. He liked the chauffeur. It was odd, but he did. The liking had been increased by the quaint, spontaneous little outburst just before they left his room. But Hilling's soul remained his own, and if it wavered he only had to think of the philosophy of Polonius.

Therefore he performed an audacious act. He bent forward and slid the glass panel open again.

"This much I insist on knowing!" he exclaimed. "Are you taking me home?"

"No," said the chauffeur, and slid the panel to again.

They traveled on. For how long? Hilling lost all count. He also lost all recognition of locality. The twisting and turning, which continued throughout the journey, the fog, and the confused state of his own mind, played ducks and drakes with time and space.

They might be traveling north, or south, or east, or west. He had no idea. They might have been journeying for minutes or hours or months. He had no idea. It dawned upon him that he was probably intended to have no idea. In which case, he reflected gloomily, where was that precious thing called trust?

He was just beginning to resign himself to a condition of eternal transit when he found that the car had stopped. He did not remember it stopping—it must have done so very softly—and he only knew it had stopped by the abrupt discovery that it was no longer in motion. This was followed by the discovery that the chauffeur's back was no longer visible ahead of him. The next instant the door of the car opened, and the chauffeur's head popped in.

"Now come," he whispered.

Hilling rose, rather majestically.

"But, a moment, first," continued the chauffeur, keeping his voice very low. "Lift the top of the silver ash tray by your window. There is a key. Take it. It will open the door of the house. So open it. Go in. Close it. Wait. It is clear, yes? No, say nothing till you are inside, even when I speak. Nod or shake!"

Hilling nodded.

"Good, so! Now walk with quietness. No haste, no worry, but as you would at the Albert Hall, the great prince! Upright! Magnificent! All so fine and wonderful!"

"Damn the fellow, does he think I do not know my part?" fumed Hilling to himself, while secretly grateful for these definite instructions.

He found the key and stepped out onto the pavement.

The fog seemed thicker than ever. He could hardly see a yard ahead of him. But he made out an iron railing and an iron gate. As he strode toward them, with all the magnificence required, the chauffeur accompanied him to the gate, and made a little speech. The speech was in a foreign language, and he did not understand a word of it. He nodded, however—the flowing tide had caught him again, and he could only flow with it—and the exaggerated, over-elaborate motion of his head gave him, he thought, a momentary glimpse of another figure somewhere. Somewhere in the fog. Ten yards away? No, it could not be that. A foot? He could not say. It was gone almost before he saw it. If he had seen it at all! Perhaps he had not. Perhaps it had been merely his imagination. . . .

Hallo! What had happened to the chauffeur? He had stiffened suddenly. Where was he? Ah, there he was! No, he wasn't! . . . Gone!

Hilling stifled an impulse to call after him. It would have been the normal thing to do in normal circumstances, but the circumstances were very far from normal. A startling instinct of self-preservation kept Hilling mute.

Perhaps the chauffeur had only returned to the car. Assumedly he would have to garage it somewhere. But why such abruptness? And why that sudden rigidity? Now Hilling could see nothing. The figure or figures had vanished. The car, even at this short distance, was blotted out. . . . Yes, he could see something. The open iron gate, waiting for him to pass through. And faintly beyond, a door. The door of which he held the key.

If you had asked him, he would have said that his pause lasted ten seconds. Actually it lasted two. But in those strange two seconds the adventure into which he had been so amazingly projected took on an entirely new aspect. Unadmitted and shadowy fears began to gather around him, and to assume a terrifying substance.

He advanced to the door. That, also, grew into substance. All he could see was the door. Above it and on either side of it lay invisibility. He raised the key and inserted it in the lock. As he pushed the door inward, a brooding glow widened, and he found himself in an illuminated hall. The illumination came from a red-shaded lamp.

Suddenly the lamp cracked and went out. Stark horror gripped him. Leaping aside, he slammed the door to, and as he did so the outside wood was struck by a vicious, spitting, metallic *plop!*

Eleven P.M.

THE magic was working.

Two hours ago Henry Brown had been a poor, timid clerk, living in fear of everybody, and without sufficient authority to control an office boy. Self-conscious to a desperate degree, and with an inferiority complex that was justified by every incident he met, he had never found any escape from his sensation of slavery, or from the ingrained belief that he had been born for other people's profit. A girl would have helped him. He had had no girl. The girls he knew ignored him, and the girls he did not know were beyond his courage and his reach.

But now a new Henry Brown stood in the old Henry Brown's skin, if not in the old Henry Brown's clothes. He had not yet reached the complete emancipation that was to come; his acts of surprising daring lay still ahead. The sensation of slavery, however, had lifted from him, and the relief was like the relief from constant pain. This alone, quite apart from a glass of whisky he had drunk, imparted to his head

76

a feeling of unusual lightness. For the first time he could remember, he felt everybody's equal.

The glass of whisky, itself stimulating, had been drunk under stimulating circumstances. He had been treated to it by a man in a leopard skin. The man was only in a leopard skin, and it was a very small leopard for so big a man.

"What, not dancing, Gauguin?" the man exclaimed.

"Oh, so that's who I am," thought Henry, none the wiser, as he answered, "No—er—not just yet."

"Then we must have a drink, Gauguin," cried the man. He had obviously had several, though it was early. "Come along."

Henry hesitated. He could not bear the idea of tearing himself away from the glorious spectacle of the ballroom. He wanted to look, and look, and look. But he also wanted to make friends, and here was one, if not of the chosen sex. So he mumbled, "Well, really, that's very nice of you—thenks," and followed him.

They elbowed their way through crowds to a bar. At the bar was another crowd. They pushed forward to the counter.

"What'll you have, Gauguin?" inquired his host.

"Eh? Oh, same as you," he answered guardedly.

A few seconds later they were raising glasses to each other.

"Here's fun," smiled the leopard man.

"Cheery Honk," replied Henry dashingly.

They drained their glasses. Henry drained his too quickly, and nearly choked. While he was nearly choking, he said, "It's nice here, isn't it?" to prove he could still talk.

The leopard man's smile vanished, and he regarded Henry earnestly. In his fuddled condition he was trying to make up his mind, though Henry did not know it, whether this fellow he was treating was very profound or a damned fool. With the point undecided, he responded:

"Very nice, Gauguin, oh, very nice."

Then his hand groped about his leopard skin. "I hope he's got a pocket," thought Henry. "Otherwise, how'll he pay?" Perhaps this invitation was a trick, and Henry himself would have to pay? This would be disappointing both financially and socially, and Henry wondered whether the two florins in his own pocket would be sufficient. If not, he would have to resort to his shoe, which would be awkward in public. But it was not a trick. The leopard skin had a pocket. The drinks were paid for, and the leopard man waved good-by.

"I have to see a *very* important person," he whispered confidentially, and vanished.

The end was a little abrupt, but the incident was

satisfactory. Henry had received a light from a red general and a drink from a leopard, and if that didn't mean you were all right, what did?

He returned to the vast ballroom. It drew him with such compelling force that, as he neared the covered passage that had formed his first watching point, he found himself almost running. He pulled up sharply. He did not want to disgrace himself before the sentinel beef-eaters. He nearly knew one of them already. The one with the very long nose.

With a sense that he was home again, he took his stand in the passage, beside the beef-eater with the long nose. The ballroom by now was a familiar spectacle. He knew in which direction to look for the band. He knew where the dance numbers went up—the number was now "Five"—and where, looking upward, the biggest bunch of balloons was suspended. He knew the corner in which was an enormous Golden Shell. (He saw it in his mind in capital letters.) He knew where it was, but he had no earthly idea why it was. He even knew where to turn his head to find one particular private box. He identified it by a sort of historical chap, with a fine long wig, sitting prominently forward. A king, p'r'aps.

But although the spectacle was now so familiar, every tiny point of it tickled every tiny point of Henry Brown with the stimulation of eternal freshness.

So far he had only watched. All at once it occurred
to him that he ought to be a part of it. He had the
same right as all the other parts of it. He had paid his
one-eleven-six! True, he had not yet found a partner,
but there were plenty of partnerless people wandering
about the floor, walking in and out of the dancing
couples, some perilously losing themselves near the
center, some keeping more cautiously to the outer circle, and smiling into the boxes that encircled the great
arena like a vast populated hoop.

"Now for it!" thought Henry.

He was going to make the "grand tour." He was
about to journey round this new world. He lit a cigarette to fortify himself. The beef-eater with the long
nose eyed him. He began to advance into the ballroom. The beef-eater with the long nose stretched out
a hand and tapped his back.

"Sorry, sir. No smoking on the dancing floor."

"Oh!" muttered Henry, feeling he had committed
the unforgivable sin.

He turned. The beef-eater pointed to a little red
bucket with a thin layer of water in the bottom. Henry
threw in his just-lit Du Maurier. Bang went a half
penny! The Du Maurier joined a number of other
drowned and disappointed hopes.

"If one did it, they'd all do it," said the beef-eater.

"Quate," nodded Henry, eager to imply his appreciation of law and order without losing dignity. "Quate."

He advanced again. A couple danced into him. He dived aside. Another couple danced into him. It was worse than Piccadilly Circus! Again he dived aside and was again caught up by another couple. He went forward ahead of them, half-lifted, as though he were on a cow-catcher. The couple stopped and picked him up.

"Sorry," laughed the man.

He was wearing a tall gray top hat, and Dundreary whiskers.

"Not at all, not at all," gasped Henry. "It was my fault."

"Nothing's anybody's fault," laughed the woman.

She had a funny, ugly, stiff dress, with a bustle. The bustle had been the cow-catcher.

Henry's heart went out in gratitude to them. How kind everybody was! You *couldn't* go wrong! Perhaps that was the secret of the queer joy of it all. You couldn't go wrong! Even the beef-eater had not been really cross with him about the cigarette, and had apologized for pulling him up.

"Is that your two shillings?" inquired the man with the Dundreary whiskers.

"Eh? So it is!" exclaimed Henry, stooping and grabbing it.

"There's another one," said the woman with the bustle.

"Eh? So it is!" cried Henry.

But before he could secure the second coin somebody kicked it away from him deliberately. It slid and became lost among a maze of feet. It scored a goal somewhere.

For just one tiny instant, the golden world turned black again. Henry looked up at the person who had kicked the coin away.

"Ha, ha!" laughed the rascal.

"Ha, ha!" Henry laughed back.

He went on laughing. Two complete lunches kicked away, and he went on laughing. "My God, what's happening to me?" he wondered, while tears of merriment rolled out of his eyes. "Is it the whisky?"

"Funny little fellow," said the man with the Dundreary whiskers, as he faded away.

"Rather a nice little fellow," replied the woman with the bustle.

Feeling too near the center of the space for safety, Henry made for the circumference. He reached the curve of the private boxes. Hallo! Here was that historical king sort of chap. Still alone. He always seemed alone.

He stared at him rudely, as though he were a waxwork, quite unconscious of his rudeness. At the back of his mind was the delicious, dangerous axiom, "Nothing's anybody's fault." The historical king paid no attention to him. He was staring at somebody else. At an historical lady, dancing by at that moment with an extraordinary man in a costume composed almost entirely of pearl buttons. He did not know that, very soon, he was destined to have a closer acquaintance with them. "Hallo, Gauguin!" cried a familiar voice. "Still looking for a partner?" He turned his head to smile at the speaker, but he could not find the speaker. Instead, he found himself smiling at the girl who had smiled at him on the stairs. She smiled at him again.

"I say, I say, I must be careful," decided Henry. "I'm becoming a devil."

He moved away from the smile, trying not to feel cold as he passed out of its radius. He felt sure that this was the nicest smile of all the thousands of smiles in the hall. He drifted about like a dismembered body, wanting to attach itself, not knowing where to attach itself, or how. Now he was near the band. Its loud notes clanged in his ears. Now he was very far away from it. The notes came faintly. Now he began to feel definitely dizzy. He was convinced it was the whisky. Had the leopard man given it to him neat? He recalled he had nearly choked. He would have tossed down anything at that moment. Prussic acid. No, he mustn't take any more drink. He couldn't stand drink. He had a sudden desire for the friendly beef-eater. There was something protective, motherly, about the beef-eater. Yes, he must certainly get back to the beef-eater. Otherwise he would find himself in trouble. Funny, he felt like this. Ah, of course, he had hardly eaten anything all day. He had been saving himself up for the supper. He had gone without lunch, putting the shilling saved toward the one-eleven-six.

He groped his way toward the spot where he thought the friendly beef-eater was. He found himself in the middle of a knot of people. It was unlike the usual knot. Something was going on. He tried to get out of the knot, failed, and became inextricably tied up in it. An arm shot out. Not at him, but at some other fellow. By Jove, a fight! He must get away from it. He didn't like fights.

He saw a man on the ground. The man's lip was bleeding. The man who had knocked him down was preparing to deliver another blow. The attacker was a chap all over pearl buttons. Hey, this wasn't fair! It wasn't cricket! You couldn't hit a fellow who was already down, and whose lip was bleeding! Henry lurched forward and caught the attacker's arm. He held it with all his might. The arm remained stationary for a second, then wrenched itself away with terrible ferocity. "Now I'm going to die," thought Henry, "but I don't care." A fist hit him. He hit back. He became the center of something seething. Something that could not be worked out. The dance had turned into a game of rugby, and he was the ball. "I don't care, I don't care," he went on thinking, as he was pressed from all sides. "You shouldn't hit a man who's on the ground and whose lip is bleeding!" The beef-eater would have agreed with him, anyhow. If ever he saw that beef-eater again he would just lean on his shoulder and cry. But, of course, he would never see the beef-eater again, he would never see anybody again. Twenty arms and thirty-five legs were tied round him, and were strangling him.

Then the miracle happened. He was being pulled out. Pulled out through a hole in the human mass. He emerged from the scrum, and the scrum went on without him. It did not even know he had gone. A voice whispered in his ear, "Come away, quick, you mustn't go back!"

Go back? Don't be funny!

Now he was in the outer corridor. He did not remember getting there, though he had a vague memory of having been pulled there. But who had pulled him there? He raised his eyes and his mouth opened. It was the girl who had smiled at him on the stairs, and then again outside the box of the historical fellow.

"Take it easy," she was saying.

He blinked at her. He felt hot, and suddenly foolish and uncomfortable. She looked like a nymph. She was wearing very few clothes, but he swore it was only her face that attracted him.

"I—I expect I must look a sight," he panted vapidly.

"I expect it doesn't matter how you look," she answered. "You were damn silly to go into that mix-up."

Was she reprimanding him? He was not sure that he could stand that.

"The chap's lip was bleeding," he muttered. "And I—I hate blood."

She looked at him curiously. Her face was close. He smelt the powder on it.

"Yes—I believe you do," she said. "I believe you need looking after. Do you still want a partner—Gauguin?" He stared at her. "I heard someone call you that. Anyway, whether you do or don't, I managed to rescue *this* for you!" She held up a little flashlight, with an unusually large lamp at the end. "How it didn't get broken beats me! I expect it fell out of your pocket."

Now he stared at the light. It was, if he had known it, the most interesting article in the whole of the hall. He shook his head.

"Not mine," he murmured.

"Oh, not? Then it must have fallen out of somebody else's pocket. But we're not going back to return it, my dear! How about going up now for a bit of supper and watching the New Year in together from the top?"

He did not believe he had heard the words aright.

"What's the matter?" she asked. "Feeling queer?"

"Well—as a matter of fact—I do feel a bit funny," he answered. "Yes, I—I should like a bit of supper."

"Then whoopee, atta boy!" she cried, taking his arm with friendly intimacy. The warmth of her own arm sent him direct to heaven. "And p'r'aps we can rake up a bottle of bubbly to go with it, shall we? Look after this fancy toy, you'd better. Slip it in your pocket!"

"A spot of trouble over there," commented Harold Lankester, as he and Dorothy Shannon entered their empty box from the back and looked out into the hall across the low parapet.

"Aren't they mad!" replied Dorothy.

"Ah, you accept my theory," he smiled.

"When it comes to horse-play, yes. The rest—I don't know. In a way, I feel rather sorry for them."

"Them?"

"Touché! Us."

"That's right. Us," he nodded. "If it's a rum world, we can't individually escape responsibility. We're all a part of it." His eyes grew serious for a moment, then quickly relaxed. "Wonder what's on? It looks like a miniature war."

"Conrad will tell us," answered Dorothy. "I can see him on the edge of it. Look—he's going closer! I hope to God he doesn't make an idiot of himself and get mixed up in it!"

"Shall I go out?" asked Lankester.

"No, stay here," she responded quickly.

"Meaning you're afraid I may get mixed up in it?"

"You might."

"True. Small nations." The remark sounded cryptic, and he did not explain it. "Well, I'm quite happy where I am."

"Yes, it's nice and quiet in here."

A silence fell upon them. He gave her a cigarette, and lit one for himself. As his eyes met hers over the match, he smiled, rather uncertainly.

"Yes—it's a rum thing, life," he said. "We live it all wrong, yet can't help going on with it."

"Would you have us all commit suicide?" she answered lightly.

"I didn't mean that. Perhaps I should have said—continuing to live it wrong."

"Well, I love it," she exclaimed immediately, as though afraid of another silence.

"It has good moments," he replied. "But if you love

it, why did you say just now that you were sorry for people?"

"I said *these* people."

"And then agreed that we were a part of these people. I'm not telling you anything you don't know— am I?—when I say that all these people we are looking at are thoroughly representative specimens. They reflect our age, our condition, our laws—our necessities. That's what makes it all so interesting and real. And important. Am I boring you?"

"You never bore me."

"But—something?"

"Yes—something. Why are you so serious tonight?"

The door opened again, and Mrs. Shannon entered. She was trying heroically not to look worried.

"Oh, dear!" she murmured. "What *is* one to do with Conrad?"

Lankester rose and looked at Dorothy inquiringly. She nodded, and he turned to her mother.

"Deserted you, has he, the young rascal!" he exclaimed. "I'll bring him in."

"No, don't," she said. "It's silly to worry. And he'd hate it. He'll be all right. Where's Dad?"

"Mr. Shannon wasn't here when we came in just now."

"Wasn't he? I expect he's just wandering about. What about supper? We might have it brought in after this dance, and then we can all drink to the New Year. There, look! It's breaking up! Oh, and there's Conrad! He's coming back." She sat down, relieved. "What *do* you think of me, Harold? I'm quite ashamed of myself, because if there's one thing I disagree with, it's parents worrying."

A few moments later Conrad burst in like a large golden firework.

"Did you see it?" he cried. "It was a real scrum! One chap almost got knocked out!"

"What happened, dear?" asked Mrs. Shannon.

"Well, I didn't see the very start," he ran on, "but as far as I can gather somebody cheeked the coster about losing his partner or something. Mad hat! Why, everybody talks to everybody, and nothing means anything. Someone said to *me* just now as I came along, 'Blimy, where's me dark glasses?'"

"And you had lost *your* partner, too, hadn't you?" said Lankester, with a definite inflection in his voice.

"My partner? What do you——?" He stopped abruptly, and flushed beneath the imprisoning gold. "Oh, I say! But I thought—did you get back all right, Mother?"

"Well, I'm here," smiled Mrs. Shannon. "Go on, it was all right. And then the coster hit him?"

"Rather. A real smack. And down the poor chap

went wallop! It might have been all right—I mean, there mightn't have been any more of it—if somebody else hadn't barged in—a little chap with a beret twenty miles round and check pants——"

"I've seen him," nodded Dorothy.

"Well, he looks a prize fool, though I'm not one to talk, but he's got some pluck. I believe he was trying to rescue the chap on the ground, but the next moment he was on the ground himself, and nobody ever saw him again. I think he got pressed down to Australia. Anyhow, when they'd all disentangled themselves, he wasn't there."

"But what about the first man who was knocked down?" asked Mrs. Shannon anxiously. "Was he badly hurt?"

"Not a bit. He's dancing again. What I've always noticed about this place is that everybody's good-natured. If we'd been French or Italian, there'd have been murder, but the only one of the whole bang crowd who really lost his wool was that coster. To the rest it was just a lark."

"If that's the modern idea of a lark," remarked Mrs. Shannon, "it's more than *I* can understand! Did you see Dad anywhere, Conrad?"

"Dad? No! Isn't he here? So he isn't."

"What happened to the coster?" inquired Dorothy.

"We left him still looking. For the chap in the loud pants. He's still a bit upset, but he'll cool down. I say, what about eats? I'm getting a hole in me."

"We'll have supper as soon as Dad comes back."

"Then I'll bring him back! I don't suppose he's far off."

He was out of the box again in a flash.

Mr. Shannon was a considerable way off. He was in a corridor at the far end of the hall, cooling down after a disturbing meeting with a lady in a Nell Gwynn costume.

The meeting, of course, had been quite accidental. So Mr. Shannon assured himself. True, the lady had happened to smile once or twice while passing his box, and maybe he had smiled back, in recognition of the historical coincidence. Yes, he admitted, he had smiled back. Little things like that were nothing! Just part and parcel of the occasion, almost an obligation to the occasion. If you were going to worry over a smile or two, you had better stay at home. But he had merely left the box, after that last smile, to stretch his legs, and he had never expected that, as he stood on the fringe of the great revolving kaleidoscope of dancers, this lady would dance right by him, and drop her fan again. Naturally, he had picked it up. Naturally, she had rewarded him with another smile. And— well, if she had implied to her partner that she was tired, and if the partner had sloped away grumpily, as though dismissed, that surely was not Mr. Shannon's fault? Was it not the partner's fault for acting with such unnecessary boorishness, and for interpreting the lady's attitude in the way he did?

"Well—did you see *that?*" exclaimed Nell Gwynn, herself appearing astonished.

"I—I hope I had nothing to do with it?" murmured Charles II.

"I expect you had everything to do with it," she retorted, with disarming candor. "The jealous idiot! Just because I——" She paused and laughed. "Smiled at an old friend!"

"Old friend?" queried Mr. Shannon, purposely obtuse.

"Well, in a way, you are, aren't you?" inquired Nell Gwynn, and added, with a wicked twinkle, "Charles?" And then, while Charles swallowed, she tossed her head and exclaimed, "Who is he, anyhow? Frankly, I'm not sorry to be rid of him!"

"Isn't he a friend of yours, then?" inquired Mr. Shannon cautiously.

"Friend of mine? Gramercy, no!" she retorted. "He's been hanging round me all the evening. I couldn't shake him off. Thank you, Nell Gwynn is a little more particular! I expect he saw us looking at each other, and didn't like it."

Now was the moment for Mr. Shannon to show his strength and deny the imputation. Or, at least, to imply its insignificance. Yes, this was the moment he should have given the too-attractive lady one more smile and departed. He knew it. She, also, knew it, and watched him covertly from beneath her heavily-blacked lashes. But the moment went by, and Mr. Shannon said nothing. Nor did he move. A little door was opening in his starved soul, and he could not bear to close it.

The silence lengthened. He began to feel slightly foolish. To end the silence, and because he could not think of anything else to say, he murmured weakly:

"Did we look at each other?"

"Didn't we?" she answered. "Correct me if I'm wrong."

"I—I suppose we did," admitted Mr. Shannon. "And as it has caused this little trouble, I apologize."

"What for? Have I complained yet?"

"Well, no."

"Wait till I do, then!"

"Nevertheless," insisted Mr. Shannon, cursing himself for his rusty conversational ability and feeling that he ought to be doing this very much better, "nevertheless I feel I ought to apologize."

"You can, then, on one condition. No, two."

"What are they?"

"The first, Charles, is that you let me hear you call me Nell while you do it!"

"Eh? Well, why not. I apologize, Nell."

The sound of the name on his own lips gave him a disturbing little thrill. "Come, come, this mustn't continue," he thought to himself. But he asked, "And the second condition?"

"That you go on doing it," she laughed, and then suddenly seized his arm. "I say, what's happening over there? A free fight? Let's get somewhere clear of it!"

Still holding his arm, she led him out of the ballroom. Now they were standing in a comparatively quiet corridor. "How can I get away?" thought Mr. Shannon. "How did it all begin? I was a fool! This won't do, you know! I must go right back to my box."

As though in answer to his thoughts, her voice penetrated his confusion.

"But, of course, you're with a party, aren't you? Lucky man. I'm not."

"Unfortunately—I mean, yes, I am with a party."

She gave a tiny sigh. It was the prettiest compliment. She regarded him thoughtfully for a moment, then dropped his arm and held out her hand.

"Then I mustn't keep you, Charlie. But it would have been nice if we could have done a bit of exploring together. It's an interesting building. Good-by."

He took her hand.

"Or, perhaps, just *au revoir,*" he answered, feeling idiotic.

"Well, if you're lonely any time," she said, "this is where you'll probably find me."

She squeezed his hand, walked away, threw him a final smile over a dazzling shoulder, and vanished.

Mr. Shannon took a deep breath. He knew he had behaved very foolishly and unwisely. But he did not know whether he were sorry or not.

He turned in the opposite direction. After a few paces he stopped. Something was trickling down his forehead. He raised his lace handkerchief and wiped his forehead. He realized that it would never do to return to Box 12 in this condition. He sat down on a sofa to cool.

And there, a trifle too soon for his convenience, his son found him.

"I say, Dad, you look *hot!*" exclaimed Conrad. "Were you in that scrum?"

On the point of asking, "What scrum?" Mr. Shannon changed his mind and answered, "Yes."

Sally now had two potential meeting places in the Hall. The first was the spot she was leaving. The second was a sheltered recess on the first balcony.

She walked leisurely to the second. There she

waited. Her eyes were no longer laughing and flirta-
tious; they were grim, almost brooding. This was not
merely because her job was giving her little pleasure;
it wasn't much fun hooking a poor, easy fish like Mr.
Shannon. It was because an indefinable anxiety lay in
her heart, an uncomfortable sensation that things were
not going right. Menace hung in the air, and almost
for the first time in her life she was afraid. The fact
that she did not know exactly why was no alleviation.

"Of course, Sam was a bad bloomer!" she confessed
to herself. "I ought to have got someone else. His
mood's all wrong, and if he bungles we're done for—
and good-by to my two hundred!"

Well, he *mustn't* bungle! She would have to see
to that. When he came along she would have a
straight no-nonsense talk with him, and if he looked
like making trouble. . . .

He came along at that moment, with trouble written
all over him. His face was dark.

She attacked him at once. She wanted to cow him,
to force him to follow her mood instead of allowing
him to force her own. She knew the danger of losing
her ascendancy.

"*You've* made a nice start!" she said.

He looked at her in surprise. How the devil did she
know? An instant later he realized that she had not
meant what he meant, and that she did not know.

"Making a scene like that!" she went on, admonishingly. "If you're going to get what you hope out of this, you'll have to watch that temper of yours!"

"What do yer mean?" he retorted, deciding to clear up the lesser evil before referring to the greater, which would not be so easy to clear up. "I sloped off when that blinkin' fool come along, didn't I, like was agreed?"

"You sloped off all right!"

"Corse I did! Down goes your fan fer the signal. Fool picks it up. That was my cue fer gettin' 'uffy and leavin' yer, wasn't it? All right, then. I did get 'uffy and leave yer, so what's the complaint?"

"The complaint is exactly what you've just said," replied Sally. "Just exactly! You got huffy and left me. You didn't *pretend* to get huffy and leave me. You *got* huffy! And then you lost your head and went off and made a silly scene!"

He frowned. He knew he had lost his head, and he knew he had really got huffy. But he wasn't really the sort of fellow to stand nonsense from any man; he never had been and he never would be; and this play-acting before a lot of fools stuck in his stomach. Sally was *his* girl! Had been once, anyway, and was going to be again, if he knew anything about it. He had wanted to biff the stupid old josser on the nose. Instead, he had had to slope off like a timid schoolboy.

And then somebody who had noticed the incident had followed him, and chipped him about losing his girl before the crowd. Naturally, he had struck him!

He was about to explain all this and to justify himself when he altered his tactics. Why should he explain? That was another thing about him. He never explained. Certainly not to any girl! If Sally had been any other girl he would soon have sent her about her blinking business! So, instead of offering an explanation which (he well knew) would not have been accepted in any case, he launched a counter-attack.

"Well, was *you* pertendin'?" he challenged.

"What's that mean?" she retorted.

"That Charles II, I don't think!" he said.

Her eyes blazed.

"By God, Sam, it's true, you *don't* think!" she flashed. "If you did, you'd know I could never fall for a boob like that!" ("Nor for you, either!" ran on an unspoken thought.) "Flabby fifty! Thank you very much! I must be hard *up!*"

In the pleasure of this spirited denial, and in his ignorance of the unspoken thought, Sam felt better.

"Oh, well, don't let's quarrel," he muttered. "Ferget it! Goin' all right with 'im, eh?"

"Easy."

"I said it would be. When you get among 'em, you don't need no bait."

"Leave me to do my part of it. The question is, can you do *yours*?"

She noticed the sudden twitching of his features. Her remark had slapped his memory back to something he would rather have forgotten.

"What's up? Why don't you answer?" she exclaimed. "What are you staring at?"

"Well, the fact is, Sally——" he began.

But she pulled him up with a quickly whispered, "*Cave!*" Then, as someone passed, she laughed and cried, "What, right into the orchestra? It must have been a scream!"

When they were alone again, Sam mumbled, "That blinking Balkan bloke's everywhere!"

"Yes, isn't he?" answered Sally quietly. "Well, go on. Let's have it. The fact is——?"

"Eh? Oh!" He hesitated, then plunged. "The fact is, I—I've had a bit of bad luck."

"Oh?"

"Yus."

"Go on."

"I am, ain't I? I've lost my little flasher."

She looked at him as though she wished he were dead. But her voice remained quiet. It was like cold steel.

"I guessed something like that would happen," she said. "Right, wasn't I?" She waited while two people ran by, chasing each other. "In the scrap, I suppose?"

"That's right."

"Fell out of your pocket?"

"That's right."

"Both your little flashers?"

He looked uncomfortable, but her eyes were piercing him too sharply for prevarication. They were like cold steel, too.

"I only 'ad one," he said.

"And you wonder why you're going down, while I'm going up!" she blazed, forgetting her caution for an instant, her voice louder with fury. It dropped again, however, as she went on, "I told you to bring two. Why didn't you?"

"I sat on one."

"You'd be a good one to bring up pups! You sat on one, and you've lost the other. And now, we're done!"

"There you are, lookin' on the worst side at once," he grumbled, trying to imply a weakness in her armor to divert attention from his own. "We can find it again, can't we?"

"I believe somebody once found a needle in a haystack," she retorted.

"Yus, by *lookin'* for it," he pointed out.

"Oh, yes, we'll look for it," she answered bitterly. "But I suppose you've done that already?"

"Made a start. Then I stopped to come 'ere to you."

"Suppose somebody has sat on the one you've lost?"

"I ain't supposin' it."

"You ought to be a weather prophet, the way you keep your optimism! Why don't you suppose it?"

" 'Cos I think I know 'oo's got it."

"You do?"

"Ain't I tellin' yer?"

"Who?"

"A chap in the scrap. Suddenly 'e joins in, and seizes me arm. And down we go together, with the lot on top of us." He paused and thought. "Yes, I'll swear 'e's got it."

"Go on, go on," she exclaimed impatiently. "Why do you think he's got it?"

"Well, 'e wasn't there afterward. 'E'd skermoosed! Not a sign of 'im. And, if the thing 'ad broke, I'd 'ave seen some of the pieces."

"Sure there were no pieces?"

"Not on the ground, and not in me pocket."

Now Sally thought, and all at once her lips tightened.

"I wonder if you've walked into it, Sam?" she said. "Right into it, like a dear little lamb? I wonder whether this has been a put-up job? Scrap and everything!"

"You mean——"

"I mean there's more hangs on this than you guess, as I've told you before. There's the hell of a lot! There may be people here who are working against us——"

"Yus, more than I guess!" interrupted Sam warmly. "And who makes me guess? You don't tell me *nothing!*"

"When it comes to knowledge, Sam," she responded scornfully, "you're best spoon-fed. Now, then. Let's straighten this out. Somebody gets your dander up—on purpose. You go for him, and knock him down. Then another fellow comes along. Working together, of course. And while the trouble's on, he slips the thing out of your pocket, and bolts. What were they like? We've got to find those two men, Sam! What were they like?"

"I can't remember the first one," answered Sam. "It was all too quick. I just 'eard 'is voice be'ind me, and I swung round and 'it 'im. I think 'e was dressed like a sailor, but there's dozens of sailors. And then, you see, I was switched off to the second chap. I remember *'im*, though. And 'e's the chap we want. You could 'ardly see 'is face fer 'is 'at—one 'o them berrys, you know, sloppin' all over the place—and trousers—well, slacks, more—that give yer a 'eadache——"

"Checks?" interrupted Sally, her eye brightening. "Loud checks? And a dark velvet jacket?"

"What, you know 'im?"

"I've seen him! Once seen, never forgotten! I heard somebody calling him Gauguin."

"*I'll* never ferget 'im, either," muttered Sam, "and when I find 'im I'll give 'im something 'e won't never ferget!"

."Yes, well, shut up for a moment!"

"Why?"

"I'm thinking!"

Hell, she was a tartar! But he waited, and she kept him waiting only a few seconds.

"Now, listen, Sam," she said. "It's not going to be easy to comb this whole place. We may be lucky, but we may not be, and if I'm right and he's working against us, that means he won't be any too prominent. And it means another thing—it means we're being watched. You're quite certain you'll know him again?"

" 'Ow many times 'ave I got to say a thing——"

"Yes, yes, quieten down! I'll keep my eyes open down below, and you search from this floor upward. It goes upward for a mile, but we can't help that. And, anyway, I can't leave the floor for long because I've got to hang round there to meet my idiot. In fact, I ought to be getting down now. He may pop out of his kennel to find me at any moment. So get busy, my clever boy—and if you find Gauguin and bring back what he's got, I'll forget the past, and we'll start fresh."

Sam nodded.

"I'll find 'im," he said. "I'll find this Gogang! And I'll make 'im wish 'e'd spent the night at the Zoo."

"Take my advice and cut out the rough stuff," she retorted. "A bit of quiet pickpocketing is what we want now—which is just about your limit!"

"Is it?" grunted Sam indignantly. "Well, you get down to your business, and I'll get on with mine. As fer the pickpocketin'—I'll think about it. This feller may 'ave come in as Gogang, 'ooever that is, but 'e's goin' out as Gogang's corpse!"

Later in the evening, Sally recalled the boast with a shudder.

Warwick Hilling did not like it. He did not like it in the least. He possessed the average amount of courage, and at moments of crisis he was able to draw upon the poets and philosophers. "A coward dies many times before his death, a hero dies but once," had fortified him on many an anxious occasion, and his last thought before being operated on for appendicitis had been, "Fear is more pain than is the pain it fears." But philosophy is not of much use when you are standing in the dark hall of a totally unknown house, have just seen a lamp smashed by a bullet from the street, and have heard another patter against a quickly closed front door.

He stood for a few moments perfectly still. There seemed nothing else to do. He waited for the sound, or perhaps the feel, of a third bullet, or for some other demonstration from the invisible enemy. Nothing more happened. The utter silence of the fog-bound house was broken only by the thumping of his own heart.

Then, his first panic spent, he began to collect his scattered wits. Until now his strange job had been comparatively easy. His not to question why, his but to do or—— He avoided the final word of the quotation. Instructions had been given to him, and he had simply carried them out. Now, however, something had gone wrong with the plans, there was something very definitely awry, and it became necessary to rely on his own rather benumbed initiative.

The thought that he had been deliberately trapped did not occur to him. If he had few friends, he had no enemies. He was convinced, moreover, that although harm might come to him, the little chauffeur meant him none.

He was facing the front door which he had closed. It was, happily, a stout wooden door, and the small fanlight above it looked opaque. Should he turn and

explore the hall, switching on another light somewhere? There must be a switch inside one of the other
doors. Or should he open the front door again to
investigate?

Only one argument urged the latter course. It was,
however, rather a strong argument. The chauffeur.
Did he need help? Had he been hit?

The idea worried him. It became insupportable. He
decided he must risk it.

He minimized the risk as much as he could by
remaining well on the inside of the front door as he
opened it, following its short, curved course back-
wards. With the door wide open, and himself well
behind it, he waited. "I'll count ten," he thought. He
counted very slowly, the slowness increasing as the
number mounted. Then, caution exhausted, risk had
to be endured. He stepped out of his protection into
the yawning aperture.

Now he was on the front doorstep, a mark for a
third bullet. As there was no light behind him—a
comfort, that—and as he could see no one in the fog
ahead of him, a successful shot would have to come
from very close quarters. It would be preceded, assumedly, by a sudden, swift disturbance of the fog. A
quick blotch, a bit of a figure, a hand. Well, if it came
quickly like that, perhaps *he* could be as quick, too!

Again he waited. Again he counted ten. Then,

leaving the door just ajar, he stepped out into the fog, and up to the iron gate, and onto the pavement.

Yellowness. Silence.

He advanced cautiously to the curb. Here he expected to find the car. There was no car. It had gone.

And now came a short period of horrible indecision. He really did not know what to do; where his duty lay. The simple panacea for British trouble, "Find a policeman," did not seem so simple in these particular circumstances. In the first place, where would he find one? In the second place, if he did find one, what should he tell him? He did not feel he was happily dressed for the interview, and British policemen, for all their worth, are not imaginative. In the third place, would the little chauffeur (if still alive, and so far Hilling had not tripped over the body) want him to bring a policeman into it? In other words, could Hilling yet regard himself as a free agent, having earned his fifty pounds and completed his job?

He had been told to go in and wait. . . .

He turned back from the empty curb. Mr. Britling had seen it through. Mr. Hilling would see it through.

While he retraced his steps to the front door he became uncomfortably conscious of his back. It felt cold and unprotected, and it received a number of imaginary bullets in a number of different places. The worst place was just under the back of his neck. He forced the next flight of fancy lower down.

"Was I wise to leave the door ajar?" he wondered, as he reached it. "Somebody may have slipped in."

In that case, he argued, desperate for comfort, the door would surely not *still* have been ajar? It would have been closed, or wide open? Surely? Unless, of course, the person who had slipped in had been very subtle, and had desired Hilling to follow this very line of thought and shed thereby his caution.

"I cannot pretend that I like this," reflected Hilling, as he pushed the front door open and entered the silent house a second time.

He liked it even less when he heard a sound from the back of the hall. Somebody *had* got in!

He closed the front door quickly. It closed with a dull, muffled bang. He closed it for two reasons. One was to prevent himself from the indignity of bolting out of it again, and the other was to prevent anyone else from bolting in. He could not deal with a frontal attack if he were also attacked from the rear.

Now there was silence again, saving always for the thumping of his heart. The thumping annoyed him, even through his frank terror. "What is this?" he demanded of himself. "Am I not a man?" He might perhaps have urged in his defense that he was a man with a rather empty stomach.

The sound from the back of the hall started again. The cause of the sound was painfully obvious. The somebody who had got in was creeping softly toward him. Realizing suddenly that immobility would not serve him, Hilling slipped aside. Luck favored him. He slid into an open doorway. Behind him was a dark room. His hand moved about for the electric light switch. Ah! Good! Here it was! He felt it comfortingly with his fingers, rejoicing in the slight coldness of the metal. Any moment now he could produce a flood of light. But his fingers hesitated. The person in the hall was still advancing, and if Hilling turned on the light now he would reveal his advantage and perhaps gain nothing from it. Better wait a few seconds, maybe, until the person had advanced to the doorway, and was within reach. Then on with the light—give him a surprise—and spring!

And so it happened. The person continued to steal forward, and now the sound of his breathing was added to the sound of his footsteps. Here he was! A vague movement in the darkness. Up went the lights, and, with a ridiculous roar, Hilling sprang.

His arms went round the small figure of the chauffeur.

"Ei! Ei!" gasped the chauffeur.

"My God!" gasped Hilling.

As he let go, and the chauffeur slid to a sitting position on the floor, he began to feel a little hysterical. He started to titter.

"Oh! It is funny?" choked the chauffeur, though more in reproach than anger. "Good, so?"

"Not quite so good, so!" panted Hilling, and leaned against the wall.

They gave each other a full minute to recover. Then the chauffeur rose slowly, and Hilling noticed a red mark on his wrist. The sight sobered him.

"Did I do that?" he asked.

"No, you did not do that," answered the chauffeur, with a pale smile. "As you say, Mr. Hilling, it is not so good, so!"

They entered the room that was now illuminated. Instinctively Hilling glanced toward the window, then dashed for it and pulled down the blind. The chauffeur, rapidly reviving, emitted a little chuckle.

"That is wise, yes," he commented. "You show yourself, good. And now you do not show yourself, good. Well, we are here. A drink, do you agree?" He smiled grimly. "For soon it is the New Year!"

He went to a small cupboard. The room was an elegantly furnished sitting room. But Hilling wanted something before the drink. He wanted information.

"How did you get in?" he asked.

"By the back door, and by the key of the back door that I have," answered the chauffeur. "And you?"

"But you know that!"

"Pardon, I do not know yet what I know! I think you are in. Then I think you are out. Then you come in again, but I do not know it is you till you have me in the circle-grip. When you are in once, how is it that you come in twice?"

Briefly, while the chauffeur produced the drinks, Hilling related the circumstances. The chauffeur listened intently, then he nodded.

"You do well, Mr. Hilling," he said. "I see I make no mistake about you. 'He is good, as well as he is clever,' I say. 'He has the sense of honor!' And so it is! Drink, my friend!" He handed over a glass. "And then we eat. Perhaps the eat should be before the drink, but it is a big moment, this, so no matter, we drink to it! I drink to you, Mr. Hilling!" He drained his glass. He put it down. His eyes grew a little tearful. "Do you know why I drink to you, my friend? I tell you. I understand more than you tell me. Oh, yes. You are in here, and the bullets fly, and the door is close. Good. But you go out again. For me!" He thumped his chest. "I am hurt, perhaps. The risk, for me!" He poured out another glass. "Then, once more, I understand. I am one that understand much. The terror. The joy. The love. The hate. And—ha, ha! The English policeman! Am I right, so? Do you not think of the policeman?" He drained the second glass. Hilling watched him, fascinated, as he filled the glass a third time. "But you do not fetch the policeman. And you do not run away. You come back. You think, 'My God, but the Duty,' and you come back. Do I not read the mind? And, because you go out, you are brave, and because you come back, you save all, and I embrace you!" He drained the third glass, leaped forward, and kissed Hilling on each cheek. Then, as he fell back, he looked a little sad and ashamed. "Bah, do not attend to me! It is the emotion! I, too, have been in a funny time with the bullets. You will bind the hand, good, so?"

He whipped out a large handkerchief with his left hand and held out his right. Hilling took the handkerchief mechanically and bound the wrist. He bound it without speaking. He had been drowned in a sea of words. Then something burst inside him, and he cried, suddenly and despairingly:

"Yes, yes, yes! But in heaven's name—in heaven's name, *what is it all about?*"

The little chauffeur was staring at his bandaged wrist. For a few moments he continued to stare at it. When he looked up his eyes were quiet again. His passages from one emotion to another were swift and disconcerting.

"It is about a statue," he said. "A statue that will be made one day in the so soon New Year, in a place I know. Me, I see that it is made. But who is the statue, you ask? I tell you. It is the statue of Mr. Hilling."

MIDNIGHT

To FEEL the sensation of the Chelsea Arts Ball you must be on the dancing floor. You must mix with the dancers, revolve with them, become a part of the kaleidoscope. You must hear their voices and their laughter, and the rustle of their clothes, and the swish of their feet like a great whispering tide; and the music, too—you must listen to that, now loud as you draw near it, now fading as you draw away from it, now hardly audible above the whispering tide of feet. The music is stationary. The tide moves with you. Close your eyes, and you are on a strange shore. Open them, and you are on a stranger. The shore of conscious life, swept by human attraction. And you must catch wisps of scent and of lovers' remarks, sniffing or listening with good-humored impertinence; and you must bump into people. Oh, certainly, you must bump into people! But, being of the Chosen, always with honorable intentions. And whatever you do, or whatever is done to you, you must not care a damn.

But to *see* the Chelsea Arts Ball, you must be high

up. The higher you climb, the more your view will improve.

From the boxes on the first tier you will look down on heads and headdresses with the sensation that you could stretch out your hand and almost touch them as they go by. This is an illusion produced by the fact that, although you are well above them, compared with the complete altitude of the enormous hall you have hardly climbed at all. There is still far more space above you than below you, and without much difficulty, after a bottle of Heidsieck, you could let yourself over the low red-plush parapet, drop into the box immediately beneath you, and be on the floor in a matter of seconds.

From the boxes on the second tier, which is the highest tier of boxes, you find yourself more distinctly separated from the ground. Now you would need several bottles of Heidsieck to risk the descent. You exclaim as you enter the box, to compensate for your disappointment in having applied too late for the more popular boxes on the lower tiers, "Hallo, *this* is the spot to see it from!" There is some justification for your exclamation. Already, at this altitude, the bird's-eye view is beginning to dawn. You watch groups of people instead of individual people. If you suffer from vertigo you may feel a little giddy. But you have not yet found the spot to see it from.

Above your head, in the third, penultimate circle, are people who have paid less for a better spectacle. You need not envy them, however, for they are barred from participation, and must stay where they are put. They are not in fancy dress, or even in evening dress. They have paid five shillings to feast their eyes, to admire, to criticize, or to envy, and to go home afterward to express their admiration or criticism or envy. They have ascended by back ways and cold stone steps, like poor relations. But they are quite happy. They were not forced to come. They get their money's worth. Toward midnight they bring out bottles of their own, or buy cups of coffee, and smile at one another as one year goes and another comes. And they, also, say, "This is the spot to see it from!"

But they, also, are wrong. The spot to see it from is at the very top, in that great last circle that glimmers in the clouds like a vast halo.

The halo is dotted with supper tables. They extend round its complete curved length. And here you sit, unless you are having your supper cooped in one of the boxes, looking down at the Chelsea Arts Ball, and seeing it in all its bewildering completeness.

The dancers look like brightly colored ants. Moving, revolving, changing. Or like a colored ocean, with tides of different hues. You can watch the tides, and see how they are flowing, while those who form the tides are in ignorance. Here comes a current, sweeping inevitably and mathematically toward a little stationary group. You can see that the ants in the stationary group must be swept up in it; but they do not. Now they are caught—spraying away—startled and laughing. One colored ant falls over. Another pulls it up. Both are laughing. That you take for granted, though you cannot hear their laughter. You watch another point. You see a sudden quickening of the movement. It swells, communicates itself, flows halfway round the floor, breaks up. Now the ants are all breaking up. Something quite new is happening. Some are running to the outer edge of the whirlpool, others are floundering, others are slipping and sliding. Your eye concentrates on twenty or thirty bright yellow ants. They are trying to get together. Now they have got together. Now they have formed a line, and are pulling and pushing something in their center, on the top of which is perched a special yellow ant. The thing they are pushing and pulling, and on which the special ant is sitting, is an enormous golden shell. . . . The great organ, concealed behind its camouflage of clouds, rolls forth. . . .

"What's happening?" whispered Henry Brown.

"Stunts," replied the sparsely-clad nymph who sat opposite him.

"Stunts?"

"Art Schools. Every year the Art Schools make them, and shove them round." She looked at him amusedly, half-curiously. "You've not been to one of these shows before?"

"Eh? No, this is my first," he admitted. "But it's not going to be my last!"

"Good for you!" she laughed, and poured out his second glass of Perrier Jouet.

The Perrier Jouet would cost Henry a guinea. Twenty-one lunches! But he had not had the courage to order Famiray et Fils, which would have cost him only fifteen lunches. To her credit, she had done her best to make him.

"What made you come?" she asked.

"I don't know," he answered. "I'd heard people talk about it."

"And wanted a spot of the gay life?"

"That's it."

She raised her glass, and they drank. The wine percolated through him dizzily. She was not quite so distinct as she had been, but she was ten times more desirable.

"What made *you* come?" he inquired.

"Same thing, I expect," she replied. "But I'm an old bird."

"Oh, come! Not so old a bird!"

"Guess how old, then?"

"I'm no good at guessing."

"Funk it?"

"Yes. No. Twenty."

"Thank you, dear," she smiled. "You can add two." Perhaps she was unnecessarily truthful, but this funny little man rather interested her, and she had an impulse to be truthful with him, even over the trivial matter of a couple of years.

" 'Dear,' " the funny little man was thinking to himself. "I can't believe it!"

"Now shall I guess?" she went on. "Seventeen."

"Don't be silly!" he blushed.

"How old, then?"

"Twenty-five." He felt ashamed of his three extra years. "Getting an old man, eh?"

"Old man my hat!" she retorted. "Twenty-five's a nice age. That's what I should really have guessed."

The stunts were in full swing below, but Henry Brown had forgotten all about them. He looked at his vis-à-vis, and wondered. Wondered why she was sitting there. Wondered why he was looking at her, and why she was not minding. He had never looked at a girl for so long before. Was it wrong? Somehow he could not feel it was wrong. If she had minded, then of course it would have been different, but she didn't mind. He felt, in an odd, bewildering sort of a way, that she was letting him.

"What's going on in that funny mind of yours?" she challenged.

"I'd better not tell you," he answered.

"Married?"

"What?" He turned pink. "Good Lord, no!"

"Well, don't be so surprised about it! Engaged?"

"No."

"Then what's the harm? Once a year?"

He gave way.

"All right," he said. "I was thinking how nice you were being to me."

"Who's being nice to you?" she exclaimed. "But perhaps it's high time somebody started! Let me see you without your hat—Gauguin!" She stretched forward her bare arm and whipped the beret off. Then she nodded. "Like you better that way. Much better."

"So do I," he agreed.

"Shall I get rid of it, then?"

She made a motion as though to toss it into the hall below. She laughed at his consternation. Then she stuffed it under the table, and her hand touched his knee lightly as she did so. The touch fired him.

"Look here, I say," he mumbled. "I want to ask you something!"

"Forge ahead," she said.

"If I ask you questions, it's half your fault. I mean——"

"You mean that I proposed we should chum up," she interrupted. "That's all right with me. I'll take what's coming. I don't suppose it will kill either of us." But she added, with a sudden little doubt, "Only be sure it's nothing you're going to be sorry about afterward."

"Why should it be?"

She laughed at his expression. She knew more about him than he did.

"It's not going to be," she reassured him, almost like a mother. "Shoot!"

"It's—it's just this. What *made* you propose that we should chum up? Yes, that's it! What *made* you?"

She regarded him thoughtfully for a second or two. He did look better without the beret. Nothing to shout about, but better. And the wine, added to his obvious sincerity, gave an attractive glint to his usually dull eyes.

"Well, I'll tell you," she answered, "though there's nothing really much to tell. You seem to know so little about life—there, that's frank enough!—that I suppose you have to work everything out. I was watching you before you went into that fight. I was watching your expression. You were a bit funky, weren't you? Needn't answer. But you went into it, anyway—and I liked you for it. There! That enough?"

"Of course, I don't understand this at all," he muttered.

"Perhaps you're making too much of it," said the nymph. Then surprised herself a little by adding, "Or perhaps you're not."

They looked away from each other, and stared down into the hall. The golden shell had completed its journey, and was now drawn up at the side and being broken to bits. The colored ants swayed toward it, heaved away from it, climbed up on it, toppled down from it. At first Henry thought another row was on, and a pang of indignation shot through him at this work of destruction. That golden shell must have taken many days to make, and now a lot of excited, thoughtless people were smashing it! But then he noticed that the bright yellow ants, the ants who had pulled and pushed it along, were helping to smash it up. Later, his companion explained to him that it was all a part of the game. The stunts were made for the occasion, made to be smashed up immediately after their brief moment of glory. They were of no use afterward, but the space they occupied was. Meanwhile, another procession was organized, and was being pushed and pulled round the hall. The officiating ants, this time, were sea-blue, and their chariot

was in the form of a large breaking wave. It was followed by a cubic effigy of Neptune sitting on a rock.
Neptune's rock bumped into another rock, nearly dis-
placing a bunch of mermaids. A high diving board,
with a group of bathing beauties, raced perilously
around, to the sound of applause and the throbbing
of the organ. . . .

"Nearly midnight," said the nymph in Henry's ear.
How much prettier she was, thought Henry, than all
the others! Nearly every pretty girl there was prettier,
to someone, than all the others. "Glasses ready!"

He felt hot. He pulled his handkerchief out of his
pocket, and something came out with it. It was the
little flashlight with the unusually large glass bulb
at the end. He had forgotten about it.

"Be careful, or it'll go off!" she warned him.

"It's only a flashlight, isn't it?" he answered.

Suddenly he thrust it toward her, trying to flash
it in her face. He wanted to make her laugh, and to
see the light fall on her features. She ducked. But
no light came.

"Funny," he said. "It seems to be locked or something."

"Well, you put it back in your pocket," she retorted. "I don't like the look of it."

As he did so, a frown came into her face, and she
sat very still. Henry, busy with his pocket and his

handkerchief, did not notice the frown, nor did he notice the coster with whom he had fought strolling leisurely in their direction.

He was still mopping his forehead as the coster drew level with their table. The coster paused for a moment. Henry's head looked very different without his ridiculous beret. His conspicuous legs were also tucked under the table. The coster passed on. . . .

"What's up?" asked Henry.

"Nothing, darling," replied the nymph, "only I'm feeling a bit hot myself. Toss over the handkerchief!"

The nymph was a wise little person. She had not liked the looks of that coster when she had lugged Henry away from him. That was one reason why she had got rid of the beret.

"Three minutes to twelve," she remarked, as she handed the handkerchief back. "Now for some fun!"

"Do they do anything?" inquired Henry.

"Bound to be something. There'll be pipers, anyway. Listen to the corks!"

Fresh bottles of champagne were being opened all around them, in anticipation of the Big Moment. Shouldn't they have a fresh bottle, too? When purchasing the first bottle he had contrived to secure the contents of his left shoe, having surreptitiously kicked it off and then bent down as though to put it

on again; and he had one pound three shillings still in
his pocket, and two pounds still in his right shoe. He
regarded their half-filled glasses dubiously. The wine
looked sad and flat.

A waitress hovered near them, lynx-eyed. He
beckoned to her.

"No, you don't?" exclaimed the nymph.

"Yes, I do," cried Henry. "Another bottle of the
same as what we've had, and hurry your stumps!"

The waitress vanished and reappeared. She just
beat the clock.

"Pop!" laughed Henry happily, as their own cork
now flew.

There was a rustle of expectation. In the excitement of the moment and the strange illogical tension
of it, neither Henry nor his companion noticed two
figures strolling toward their table. One was Henry's
first acquaintance, the man in the leopard skin. The
other was the coster, returning.

People were standing up. Henry followed suit. So
did the nymph as he raised his glass to her.

"Not before the moment," she said. "That's unlucky!"

"O.K.—but immediately afterward," he replied.
"You know—I've got a feeling—this is going to be
some *year*!"

She smiled at him. The man in the leopard skin,

a few paces ahead of the coster, was now within a foot or two of their table. He stopped suddenly, and amused recognition entered his face.

"Why, hallo, Gauguin!" he cried. "Lost your hat?"

The coster's head swung round, and his eye glinted. Then all the lights went out.

A swift babel of voices was succeeded by an equally swift hush. For the first moment since the great hall had opened its doors to the throngs now gathered inside it to honor the new year, it contained absolute quietude. But all at once, from the minute spot occupied by Henry Brown, the silence was broken by the sound of a splintered wineglass.

Far below, in the darkness of Box No. 12, Mr. James Shannon sat and thought.

Across the big blacked-out space ahead of him things were happening. A dawning grayness began to assume shadowy shapes. The shapes shifted, expanded; they grew lighter and more distinct. They became clouds, floating about the vast screen of the sky. Then the clouds glinted with radiance at their lowest edges. The radiance spread. The rim of a large rising sun appeared, sliding upward and turning the clouds pure gold as the first *clang* of Big Ben vibrated through the ether on wireless waves. . . .

"Happy New Year!" whispered Mrs. Shannon.

But Mr. Shannon did not hear. Neither did his eyes see. They were turned inward, contemplating the bewildering chaos of his mind.

"What has happened to me?" he demanded of himself, again and again. "I have never given 'way like this before! I am James Shannon, senior partner of Shannon, Shayle and Co. I *am* Shannon, Shayle and Co.! Shayle doesn't count. My firm made munitions in the last war. It is making them now—for the next. I have just completed a very big order. A most important order. The stuff goes off the day after tomorrow entirely through my personal skill and organization—and in spite of a threatened strike. Who averted the strike? I did! I smashed it and sacked the ringleader and half a dozen hot-heads. Damned, paid Bolshies! Yes, and sacked the fool of a foreman, too, who engaged them. Why, but for me they'd have blown the place up! But I beat 'em—I don't stand nonsense—and instead of being delayed, here am I two days ahead of the scheduled date. . . . And now, hell, a mere woman. . . ."

The mere woman's face rose before him, blotting everything else out. She was beautiful, but that was the least part of Mr. Shannon's difficulty. There were thousands of beautiful women in the world. One passed them every day. This woman was not merely beautiful, however. She was also accessible.

"Stop, stop!" shouted his thoughts. "Do you hear?
Stop! Quite apart from your business, you are a respectable married man. Your name stands high, and
is going to stand higher. Any day now there will be
an announcement in the *Times* that your daughter
is engaged to a rising member of Parliament. And
the knighthood, don't forget the knighthood. Strong
probability of that. Almost a certainty, if——"

If what? If he stayed in this box, and refused to be
tempted out of it?

Come, come! He rounded on his fears. They were
ridiculous, childish! He was exaggerating the importance of the woman and the significance of the
incident. Making a mountain out of a molehill. Of
course he would not really leave his box to hunt for
this rather-too-forward young person, but what harm
could come of it even if he did? Would anyone please
tell him that? Damn it all, couldn't he be trusted to
look after himself?

Imagining himself cool and sane again, he reflected:
"I wonder if she was serious? I wonder whether she
really meant to hang around that spot? Whether she's
there now, at this moment? I don't suppose so. I
don't suppose so, not for an instant. It might be rather
amusing, though, to find out?"

He pictured himself walking along the corridor—
some time or other—to the spot. He decided that she

should not be in 'the picture. But she was. Vividly.
Beautiful, warm, and yielding. . . .

"A happy New Year!" repeated Mrs. Shannon.

"Eh?" he jerked.

What was happening? The lights were up again,
and the hall had become a mammoth playground.
People were sliding about the floor, joining hands,
romping, forming processions, galloping, calling out
to one another. And, threading through them, were
Scottish pipers. Appalled that this transformation
could have occurred without his noticing it and almost
terrified by his abstraction, he seized a glass and
clinked it boisterously against his wife's.

"A happy New Year!" he cried. "Ha, ha, ha! A
happy New Year!"

The rather-too-forward young person was not waiting for Mr. Shannon at that moment. She knew it was
a moment when his family would be claiming his
presence and attention, and that he would not be able
to slip away to the trysting place for some while. She
was therefore waiting at her second trysting place
while Big Ben chimed in the new year and the people
went mad. She heard them through walls. Heard
their shouts and their singing. They were singing
"Auld Lang Syne," their voices growing in volume.
Then, regardless of discord, the thin, nasal notes

of the Highlanders broke in, swelled, and fought for dominance. The ill-matched sounds, each refusing to yield to the other or to merge, jangled her nerves, and she stuck her fingers in her ears.

"Same here," said a voice.

It must have been very close for her to have heard. She turned her head and found a Chinaman smiling at her. She removed her fingers from her ears.

"Horrible, isn't it?" remarked the Chinaman.

"Well, no one would call it pretty," she answered.

"No one," he agreed. "Gets on one's nerves. One should carry aspirin."

"A lot of good having nerves in this place!" she retorted.

"Ah!" he smiled. "Not having any aspirin, what about a cigarette? That might help." He held out his case, and as she hesitated, "Not opium, I assure you, madam. Solid English gaspers. I am one myself."

"One what?"

"An English gasper. I gasp at your attractive cos-, tume."

He gave a little bow. She gave him a little smile, and wished to God he would go.

"You won't?" he asked sadly, as she shook her head at his case.

"I've been smoking all night like a funnel," she explained.

He shrugged, and lit a cigarette himself. He

lingered. The singing in the distance died down, the pipers faded away. The silence grew heavy.

"Queer place, isn't it?" said the Chinaman.

"Well, that's what we come for, isn't it?" she answered, only thinly hiding her impatience.

"Yes," he nodded, "I expect so. Though perhaps *my* reason. . . . Well, anyway we are as queer as the place. Not you, perhaps, but myself, certainly. A Chinaman! Isn't it ridiculous?"

"Who are you when you're at home?" she asked, without interest.

"Who are you?" he countered. "Ah! Those are our secrets! You tell me, and then perhaps I'll tell you!"

Something had, to be done about this! The Chinaman was becoming more than a nuisance, and she did not want him hanging around when Sam turned up. She decided to test him with drastic methods.

"Please don't think me squeamish," she said, looking him squarely in the eyes, "but if you're trying to pick me up, Li Hung Chang—nothing doing!"

"Ah," he murmured, unruffled. "You are looking for somebody else?"

No Chinaman could have been more inscrutable.

"I'm not waiting for anybody!" she fired.

"Forgive me," he smiled. "I am."

She turned and walked away, making a level bet with herself that he was not speaking the truth.

But whether he spoke the truth or not, the Chinaman remained where he was for over five minutes,
smoking contemplatively and watching a series of perfect smoke rings. And when a coster in a wonderful
suit of pearl buttons descended a flight of stairs near
by and paused, he took his cigarette from his mouth
and remarked:

"She went in that direction."

"Funny, ain't yer?" retorted the coster, and, as
the Chinaman suddenly looked at him hard, turned
promptly in the other direction.

Sometimes Sam was a fool, but not always.

He traced Sally half an hour later. He looked for
her, and found her, in a spot very far from their
original trysting place, and his mood was very different from his mood at their last meeting.

"You think I'm no good, don't you?" he exclaimed,
boastfully. "Bungler, eh?" He patted his pocket. It
bulged like a cheek with an apple in it. The other
pocket bulged, too, but that bulged like a cheek with
some flatter article of diet.

"What! You've found it?" she said quickly, making no effort to conceal her relief.

"Course I've found it!" he responded, with a wink.
"Trouble with you, Sall, is that you give up too soon!"

"Do I? Well, never mind about that." She was
too elated to mind his banter. "And it wasn't broken?"

"Course not!" When matters went well, Sam took all the credit. "So 'ow's that fer two blacks making a white?"

"Two blacks?" she queried.

"Yus, two, Sally!" he chuckled. "The second one was when the lights went out! See, that was when I done it. Mark my man. Out go the twinkles. Bing! And I'm off with a New Year present! Ha, ha!"

"Let's hear about it, Sam," she said. "We'll laugh when it's all over. Where was he?"

"Up at the top. That's why it took so long. Worked my way up, see? 'Avin' supper with a tart, and lookin' all goo-goo!"

"Oh, somebody with him, then?"

"You bet there was! If 'e 'adn't been so busy givin' 'er the kiss-me-darlin', p'r'aps 'e'd 'ave 'ad an eye over fer me!"

"What was she like?"

"A real little lump o' love, with a bit o' green stuff wound round."

"Have you been drinking?"

"Like a whale, I 'ave."

"Well, you keep away from it! So she was that sort, was she? I wonder if that fellow's really come here for business or pleasure? Go on, go on! The lights are still out, as far as I'm concerned! Was there a fuss?"

"No! Ain't I told you? I got away before you could say Jim Crow!"

"I suppose you recognized him by his hat?"

"Well, if you want the fact, I didn't," he admitted. " 'Cos why? 'E 'adn't got it on. And the first time I pass 'im, 'is see-me-a-mile-off pants was tucked under the table. But when I'm comin' back, just before the clock chimes, one of 'is pals calls out, 'Wot cheer, Gogang, lost yer 'at?' Gogang, see? That was the name you told me, Gogang. 'Oo is this blighter Gogang, any'ow?"

"Don't ask me," answered Sally. "I only heard the name by accident myself. But whoever he is, I'll leave him something in my will! What was his friend like? The one *you* heard say the name?" Suddenly she added, "Was he a Chinaman?"

"No! 'Oo's this Chinaman?"

"One thing at a time. What was he *like?*"

"Only saw 'im fer a moment, the lights went out so quick. S'posed ter be a tiger or something. Animal skin."

She nodded. "I know him. That's the one I got the name from, too. Sam, get that cocky look out of your face! It's dangerous! You think you're damn clever, and I'll say you're improving, but we've had a bit of luck and it won't hurt to remember it! Luck's just put us back where we were, but it won't happen twice. It's brains now, my lad, so keep yours going."

"That's right, be miserable!" grumbled Sam. "But what I want to know is about that Chinaman! 'Oo is 'e?"

"Probably nobody," she answered, "but he got talking to me while I was waiting for you, and I didn't much like the look of him."

"So didn't I!" replied Sam.

"What! You saw him, too?"

" 'E was still there. Yus, and something—familyer about 'im——"

"Did he say anything?"

"Yus."

"What?"

" 'She went in that d'reckshun,' 'e ses."

"What did you do?"

" 'Thanks, old cock,' I said. 'I was lookin' for 'er. We're doin' a job.' "

"Silly fool, talk sense!"

"Well, you talk sense! 'Wot did you do!' Think I'm a baby in a witness-box? This is wot I did. I said, 'People wot cheek me get something they don't ferget,' and went in the other d'reckshun."

No harm coloring it a bit!

Sally thought hard. Then she said, in a voice that was firm and determined:

"Sam, we've got to get this thing over right quick.

There've been too many accidents, and I don't like it.
I don't say we've got to worry about this Chink. I
don't say we've got to worry about anybody. But I'm
not going to take any chances from this moment, and
the next time I meet my fool of a man—and I'll see
it's damn soon—I'm going right through with it.
Come along, I want to show you something."

"Wot?"

"A place I've found. The place for our job. No,
don't walk with me. Walk behind me. Just keep me
in sight. There'll be some stairs to go up and down,
and—no, wait a moment! I've got a better idea than
that! Wait a moment!"

He waited obediently. In spite of his bursts of sarcasm and his periodic attempts to assert his superior-
ity, he knew Sally had the brain, and he respected it.
That was one reason why he wanted her body, too.
She wasn't just a lump, like some of the others, and
although Sam was not over-particular, he could recognize a difference.

And he, also, wanted to get this over. It was a nasty
job. Nastier, somehow, than any job he could ever
remember. It hung over him. Its very vagueness was
sinister. He couldn't see beyond it. But beyond it, he
swore, was more than twenty pounds. Beyond it was
Sally herself, he'd see to that. . . .

"Yes, I've got it," said Sally. "We're going to start

moving right away. We've got to give a bit of a fillip to my old fool, and before I take you to the nice quiet place I've found, we're going down into the hall, and we're going to walk right before his box. You're behind me, don't forget that. You're the unwanted suitor—and stop glaring! You can do that when we get outside the box, because you're to catch up with me there, Sam, and you're to catch hold of me. Then I'll shake you off. I'll give a look at old Charlie that would melt the Lord Chief Justice. An S.O.S. that will turn his heart into jelly, and do the trick if he's wavering. I'll make him come! But before he comes you'll be tucked away in your little observation box, and you'll be waiting for me to bring him along. Now, then, Sam—is all that clear, or have I got to repeat it three times?"

"Clear as mud," answered Sam. "But there's one thing that ain't so clear, and I'd like to know it."

"What?"

" 'Ow do you *know* 'e'll come? 'Ow do you know 'e's that soft?"

She smiled, and patted his arm.

"Didn't I tell you once before," she asked, "that I had a little bird?"

" 'E's a darned knowin' little bird!"

"He made it his business to be. He got a peep into someone's private diary while he was poking about

for other things—and you can take it from me, Sam,
that Mr. James Shannon is *ripe!*"

Sam looked at her shrewdly.

"Seems to me, Sally, that little bird was a bit of a
mug," he remarked.

"What gives you that opinion?" she demanded.

"Well, didn't 'e get 'old of the diary? Wouldn't
that 'ave been enough?"

She patted his arm again—she wanted him in a good
humor—while replying:

"Getting quite a wise little bird yourself, Sam, aren't
you? Yes, it's a pity he *didn't* get hold of that diary.
But he was interrupted at the wrong moment by the
writer of it himself—and now he's out of a job. You
see, he was looking for other things, as well! Anyway, probably the diary *wouldn't* have been enough.
It was—how did my little bird put it?—'evidence of
a state of mind rather than proof of fact'—and it's
the fact you and I are after tonight—which is to be
produced out of the state of mind!"

"I s'pose *you* know wot yer talking about?" grunted
Sam.

"If *you* don't, we won't waste any more time talking about it," she answered sweetly. "Now, then,
watch me go—and then count ten, and follow!"

She walked away as she spoke. Sam counted ten,
and followed.

Warwick Hilling glanced at the ornate little gold clock that whispered on the mantelpiece. He had glanced at it countless times, and had never got any satisfaction from it. It whispered busily enough, as though it were engaged on some important secret matter, but the matter was much too secret. The hands moved slowly toward an undetermined point.

For nearly an hour the ticking of the clock had formed the only sound in the room. Occasionally Hilling shifted his feet and put his left knee over his right instead of his right knee over his left, and vice versa; or softly cleared his throat to rid it of an imagined thickness. Once, in shifting, he had kicked a little table with his foot, and the noise of an earthquake could hardly have startled him more. But, since their repast, simple but ample, of exquisite sandwiches and perfect wine, conversation had died, and the little chauffeur had sat with folded arms, as though made of stone.

What was the chauffeur thinking of? Hilling would have given much to know. The chauffeur's immobility was not due to lack of interest, or callousness. It was formed of grim control, against the inner walls of which beat hot emotions and unconquerable zeal. It was almost as though the chauffeur were afraid of his emotions, at times so tempestuously expressed, and were sitting still in order to put them to sleep.

"I wonder what he looks like in his ordinary clothes?" thought Hilling. "When not dressed up as a chauffeur?"

A quarter-past midnight. Eighteen past. Twenty-one past. Twenty-three past. Twenty-four past. What did it matter? Half-past. Twenty-seven to. Twenty-six to. What was the difference? Twenty-four to. Were they making for anywhere? Was anything, ever, going to happen again?

Into the strained boredom, the tense monotony of the passing minutes, stray thoughts entered. At first they were just stray thoughts. Such as: "I wonder whether we are in Highgate or Richmond, or Sydenham or Hounslow?" "I wonder whether a policeman has walked by while we have been sitting here?" "I wonder whether my make-up is getting sticky?" The atmosphere was certainly becoming rather stuffy as well as static. "I wonder how long it takes to turn into a fossil?" But presently, as the stuffiness increased, and the staticism brought an uneasy drowsiness, the thoughts changed subtly, and became distorted. Such as: "The eyes in that picture seem to be moving." "The clock seems to be whispering more loudly. I suppose it *is* the clock?" "The chauffeur came in by the back door, he said. I suppose he closed it?" "Funny, if the chauffeur were mad!" "He looks mad." "Is he mad?" "Is he dead?" "That chair over there

is moving!" "Eh? The room's going round." . . .
The chair advanced, and asked him for a dance. "Certainly, certainly, though I haven't danced for years.
I'm an actor, you know. Warwick Hilling. I've appeared before all the Crowned Heads, but I've never
actually danced with them. Still, of course, as I have
had fifty pounds, and am a man of honor, I will dance
with you, but don't be rough, please—I'm very tired—
my God!" . . .

His head had dropped on his chest. He raised it
suddenly. The chair was back in its corner by the
window, silently protesting its innocence. "Chairs can't
move by themselves, you fool!" came the voiceless ac-
cusation. "You've been dreaming!" Dreaming? Yes!
Very likely, very likely! The room was now as stuffy
as a grave, and the fog was getting into it. Certainly chairs cannot move by themselves . . . but
windows. . . .

He screwed his eyes tight, then opened them again.
Now he was positive he was not dreaming. And he
was positive that something had happened at the
window.

He glanced at the whispering clock. Three minutes
to one. What, three minutes to one? That was a
jump! Twenty-one minutes since his last glance. He
remembered his last glance. He had been on the point
of breaking the silence and of saying, "Twenty-four

minutes to," but the chauffeur's relentless immobility had chilled the words, and they had remained unspoken.

Yes, but he would speak now! This nerve-racking silence could not continue! He would burst if he did not tell the chauffeur about the window, if he did not pour out words to him, and receive just one word in reply, or even a tiny flickering of those motionless eyes! Some sign, however trivial and minute, to dissipate this awful, oppressive sense of loneliness—and to prove that the chauffeur was not dead!

He turned to the chauffeur. It was, he found, an effort. He stared at him. The chauffeur was just as he had been at twenty-four minutes to. Twenty-one minutes ago. No—not just as he had been. There was a difference. A subtle difference. What was it? The face looked yellow.

Hilling leaped to his feet. He touched the little chauffeur who sat so silently in his chair. He found that he *was* dead.

One A.M.

HENRY'S idea of dancing was straightforward and un-subtle. It was to keep time if you could, and if you could not to stop and start again; and since, until to-night, he had never danced with anybody whose ideas were much superior to his own, he had always main-tained a low opinion of the art.

But the nymph's ideas were considerably superior to his own. Dancing with her, he discovered, was an entirely new experience. Not only did she keep time herself, but by some strange compulsion of her body she compelled him to keep time, also, and imparted to his anxious feet a strange felicity. At his first trip, when normally he would have halted like a bus after the conductor's bell, she tightened against him with a deft turn, and he found himself miraculously up-right and still moving. "How on earth did she do that?" he wondered breathlessly.

It was not merely her capable dancing, however, that gave Henry Brown his first real taste of heaven. It was her wonderful, permitted proximity. Close to him, joining her movements to his, was a creature who every moment became more definitely the last word of desirable femininity. His simple soul was convinced that, by some miraculous fluke, by some arrangement that Fate had never intended or foreseen, he had met God's loveliest creation; and he was dancing with her without any sense of guilt or shame. The occasion was sullied by neither coarseness nor cynicism.

The lack of guilt amazed him almost more than anything. He had had a rooted idea that you always felt naughty when you were with a pretty girl. At least, when you were enjoying her prettiness. The only way to avoid the naughtiness was to look at her, not fully, but out of the corner of your eye, or as though it were by accident. Even photographs of pretty girls had to be treated with careful respect. But here he was in the close presence of naked arms and, he believed (though on this point he was not quite certain, stockings had become so deceptive), naked legs, without feeling there was anything wrong about it at all! Even when his fingers accidentally touched a little portion of warm bare back, the shock he received was not ethical.

He was floating on clouds with an almost holy awe, and it was the nymph-goddess herself who tumbled him off the clouds and brought him down to earth.

"Got a toothache?" she asked.

"No! Why?" he answered.

"You look a bit dental," she commented. "Try a smile!"

His attempt at obedience was not very successful. He boldly argued with her.

"You don't *have* to smile," he said, "when you're feeling happy."

"Well, there's something in that," she admitted. "If anybody died and left me a million pounds, I'd cry my eyes out. So you are feeling happy, then, anyway?"

"Do you want the truth?"

"When it's pleasant."

"Well, this is the truth. You may think it funny. I don't know. But I've never known anything like this."

"Go on!"

"It's a fact."

"I expect it's the wine."

"*Something's* gone to my head!"

"Oh! That champagne has certainly turned you into a good talker!"

"Wasn't I before?"

"Do *you* want the truth?"

"I'll buy it, whatever it is."

"No, I'm giving it to you for nothing. You had as much conversation in you as sheep have kittens."

"Sheep don't have kittens."

"I'm learning!" She laughed. "What do they have, Mr. Schoolmaster?"

"Now you're getting silly!"

But he laughed, too.

A moment later he stopped laughing, however, and muttered, "Blast!"

"What's the trouble now?" she inquired.

"The music's stopped."

"Clap, and see if you can make it go on again?"

He clapped hard. The heroic band resumed its endurance test. Her hand went onto his shoulder again.

"See?" she smiled. "Aren't you clever?"

"Well, if I am, somebody's making me," he responded. "Do you dance a lot?"

"Whenever I can. Do you?"

"Fancy asking!"

"You're not too bad."

"Oh!"

"Fact."

"But this isn't me dancing, it's you. You're doing the work for both of us. Only for you, I'd have been down for the count long ago. Hallo, what's the joke this time?"

"You!"

"What have I said? Or have I got the toothache again?"

"No, your face is improving. It's the funny things you come out with—when before your tongue was just a passenger! 'Down for the count!' You know, I'm sure wine *is* good for you. You ought to drink a lot more of it!"

"Of course, it don't cost anything."

"True! That's the catch. Why, just think, each of those bottles cost as much as five dancing lessons. I oughtn't have let you do it."

"Good Lord, I've got enough on me for two more bottles, if I like!" he protested, richly.

He should have said "under him"—in his right shoe.

"Well, you keep it for the dancing lessons," she advised. "If you had dancing lessons, we'd be winning the Championship one of these days."

He toyed giddily with the idea. But, of course, she wasn't serious!

"I wish you'd tell me something," he said.

"We're telling each other a lot," she answered.

"What's my worst fault? Don't mind letting me know. Dancing fault, I mean."

"You may get a shock?"

"That's all right. What is it?"

"Distance!"

"What, don't I go fast enough?" he asked.

"Oh, my God, darling!" she choked. "I didn't

mean that sort of distance! We're not a couple of race horses! *This* sort of distance!"

She pulled him closer to her. He held his breath. For a moment the warmth of her breast entered into him. He experienced her form and its softness.

Presently, through a mist formed of every color of the rainbow, he said:

"I expect you think me an awful mug, but I can't help it."

"Then why am I dancing with you?" she answered. "I could get plenty of other partners."

"I can't make out."

"Give up trying. Be satisfied." Then she added, "When men tell me they've never had another girl before, I don't believe them. I'd believe *you*!"

"It's a fact," he said.

The dance ended. They drifted to a sofa in a corridor. He gave her a cigarette, and sat silently smoking his own for a minute or two. She watched him curiously, with a kind of affectionate amusement. She was not in love with him. Behind her softness and her moments of human tenderness there was something sane and practical. She was, as she had said, twenty-two, but she knew all about life, and she could face up to it without being afraid of it. She knew how to look after herself. If there was any fear in her heart as she watched him now, it was not for her, but for him.

She watched him throw his cigarette away, half-smoked, and light another immediately afterward. She guessed something was coming, and prepared to deal with it. A man who had never had a girl before might be far more dangerous than a man who had! She was quite ready to love him a little, but, knowing her own heart, she did not want to be mean to him.

"I think I've got to say something to you," he began, at last.

"Do you think you'd better think again?" she suggested.

He was nearly frightened off, but not quite.

"You guess the sort of thing it is, then?" he murmured, staring hard at the ground. And, before she could formulate the best answer, he went on, "Well, I'm going to say it, anyhow, because it's really for you I'm saying it. Because you're being so nice to me. I don't know why you're being so nice. You told me not to worry about it, and I've tried not to. But I can't help it. I always try to work things out—little things and big things—it's a sort of a habit—and I've come to the conclusion that you're being decent to me, not because of anything to do with me, but just

because you *are* decent. Well, you see, I'm not." His
cheeks flamed. "In my thoughts, I mean. They'd—
astonish you. See, I'm keeping up this game of being
truthful. I thought at first I was all right. But then—
when—well, it doesn't matter, but what I wanted to say
was just this. If you feel you want to go on dancing
with me, instead of finding other partners, you're not
going to be sorry tomorrow for anything that happens
tonight."

His forehead was very damp. He kept very still. He
knew his intentions were good, yet he felt that he had
just said something terrible. What he did not know
was that he had said something that increased the
potential danger. But she knew, and she also sat
very still, until the music in the hall started again.

He jumped up suddenly, as though to leave her.
But she was just as quick.

"I understand," she said. "And I want to go on
dancing with you."

After the next dance they did not return to the
sofa. They sat on two seats on the edge of the dancing floor itself, just beneath the low red-plush parapet
of the private boxes.

A couple brushed by them. A china shepherdess,
smiling placidly on the rather inattentive arm of a
gold statue. Suddenly Henry recognized the gold
statue.

"Who's your boy friend?" inquired the nymph.

"Nobody I know," answered Henry, "but I saw him in a car as I was coming here. Talk about mad!"

"We're all a bit dotty," she replied. "*I* don't generally go about in half a yard of seaweed, you know!"

"What do you generally go about in?" he asked, and immediately retracted. "No, don't tell me!"

"Why not? Afraid of a disappointment?"

"No, but it's more fun guessing."

"What's the guess?"

"Princess. What's yours?"

"Jardine—when you're not Gauguin. I say, who is Gauguin?"

"No good asking me!" he grinned. "But I know this, I shan't go as him next year. Mucky costume, I call it."

"You could do better," she smiled. "How about that one over there? Russian dancer?"

Henry looked in the direction she indicated, but his eyes rested on the Russian dancer's partner, and a funny, self-conscious look suddenly entered into them.

"Hallo! And who's your *girl* friend?" demanded the nymph.

"Eh?" jerked Henry. "I don't know her, either. Fact. But, see, she was in the same car as the gold fellow."

He did not add that, when he had seen her, he had vowed to spend the whole evening striving for a second glimpse! Here, now, was that second glimpse— and it meant nothing.

"She's a stunner!" commented the nymph sincerely, and only refrained from adding, "I wish I looked like that," because she knew that it would draw an unmerited compliment. The nymph was charming and attractive, but in a beauty contest she would have stood no chance against Dorothy Shannon.

Dorothy and Harold Lankester passed by, on their way back to the private box outside which Henry and the nymph were sitting. In a moment or two, another couple passed. The man had just caught up with the girl, and was taking hold of her arm.

"Sit tight!" murmured the nymph.

For Henry was jumping up. The man was the coster in pearl buttons.

She pressed him down. Meanwhile, the coster's partner appeared to be having even more trouble with him.

"*Will* you stop following me?" she murmured, audibly. "I tell you I'm sick to death of you!"

She raised her eyes, and threw a despairing glance over their heads. Into the box behind them. Then she hurried on, and the coster slouched after her.

"I—I ought to go after that fellow!" muttered Henry.

"Don't be an idiot!" retorted the nymph.

"But—you know what happened——"

"I know what you *think* happened, but you don't know it happened! You think he smashed your glass in the dark and took that wretched thing out of your pocket! Well, even suppose he did? That would just mean that it was his, wouldn't it? So what's the worry?"

Henry frowned heavily, and looked after the coster's retreating back. "If it had been his, he could have asked for it, couldn't he?"

"Perhaps he thought it would mean another row!"

"And he made me upset the wine over your dress."

"Do it good."

"And I saw something, even in the dark, that I don't think you saw I saw. When he went for my pocket you thought he was going for me, and tried to interfere—and he hit you. You had a mark on your arm when the lights went up again."

"It's gone now, anyway," she answered lightly.

"Yes. And so's he. But that chap's a wrong 'un, I'll swear, from the word go—and I'll bet he's up to no good with that little fancy toy of his, as you called it. It wasn't an ordinary flashlight, you know. You remember, I couldn't work it. It was locked, or something. And there was a funny sort of silver paper inside the lamp."

He gave a sudden exclamation.

"*Can't* you forget it?" she begged.

"I wonder if it was some sort of a bomb?" he replied.

Mr. Shannon rose from his chair and said he thought he would go and get a drink.

"Why not send for it, dear?" suggested his wife. "The waitress is just outside."

But Mr. Shannon shook his head. "No, I'd like to stretch my legs. Getting a bit cramped sitting here so long. Don't worry if I'm away for a bit—I may take a stroll round."

As he left the box Mrs. Shannon sighed.

"Really, I can't think what's the matter with Dad tonight," she murmured. "Something's on his mind."

"Business, probably," said Lankester.

"One shouldn't bring business to a ball," retorted Mrs. Shannon. "That's his trouble, he can't forget his work, and it's certainly been heavy lately. You know, don't you, Harold, we nearly had a strike?"

Harold Lankester nodded.

"You're all wrong about Dad," interposed Conrad, with a grin. "*I* know what the trouble is. All dressed up, and nowhere to go!"

"He could dance if he wanted to," retorted Dorothy.

"But he won't, 'cos why? His wig's too hot!" chuckled Conrad.

"Conrad knows everything," observed Dorothy.

"Of course he does—he's a clever little chap," he nodded. "I'll bet at this moment he's trying to find some dark and secret corner where he can take it off and fan himself. When I brought him back from his last little stroll he was melting like buttered toast. Bags I his chair, anyway! That's the spot where you get the winks!"

"Conrad!" protested his mother.

"It is," he insisted irrepressibly. "Dad's collected dozens! Go out and give me a glad eye, Sis, will you? I'd love to see how Du Barry does it!"

"Du Barry *doesn't* do it," replied Dorothy.

"Then she jolly well ought to! Nell Gwynn does. Did you see the last one that came winging in? Real fruity!"

"Harold, can you stop him?" asked Mrs. Shannon, anxiously. "She may be sitting just outside!"

"She's not," answered Conrad, poking his head over. "She went by a little while ago, and hasn't come round again since. I keep my eyes open for that lass!" He withdrew his head. "It's that funny little fellow with the noisy trousers just below us, with his new lady-love," he reported, in conspiratorial tones. "I saw 'em parked in this spot before. Lady-love, pretty light-brown hair. Nice, cheeky little nose, and queer taste in men. Funny little fellow, lost his hat but still in his trousers. . . . Hist! Plot thickens!" His voice, still sepulchral, became charged with drama. "Funny little fellow rises. He hastens away! See him hasten away! Lady-love rises to follow. . . ."

And then happened one of the trivial incidents that lead to far from trivial results. Dorothy made a grab at her too-loquacious brother, missed him, and knocked a box of chocolates over the low red-plush parapet.

"Lady-love's departure delayed by rain of soft centers!" tittered Conrad, before Dorothy could gag him. . . .

Meanwhile Mr. Shannon walked through the long, curved corridor leading to the spot where he had met and spoken to Nell Gwynn.

He told himself quite distinctly why he was going. There was to be no doubt whatever about his motive at this stage. He was going, through a sense of duty, to clear up a misunderstanding. Nell Gwynn was obviously still having trouble with the objectionable Pearly King, and as she had passed his box she had sent James Shannon a definite glance of appeal. "Can't you help me?" the glance had said, as plainly as glances can talk. "Please, *can't* you?" Well, he could not help her. Of course he could not help her. But she would never have thrown him that despairing glance unless he had, however unwittingly, given her some right to do so—unless his attitude at their previous meeting had conveyed some wrong impression. It was a point of honor to correct that impression.

"Though perhaps," he added to himself, "*I* am the one who is under the wrong impression? I may have misread her glance. I may have exaggerated it. It may have meant nothing! Well, in that case, she will not be waiting for me. There will be no one in the little alcove round the next bend, and I shall return to my box—and that will be the end of it. So no harm can come from this in either case!"

He rounded the last bend anxiously. She was not in the alcove. If his heart permitted itself a twinge of disappointment, his head felt buoyant with relief. He had been faithful to all persons, and could now return to the security of his box and his imaginings. . . .

But the next instant he found her at his side. She had flashed out from somewhere, and had hold of his arm.

"I knew—somehow—you wouldn't fail me!" she whispered breathlessly. "I'm desperate! Quick! Quick!"

The world swam. The thing had been too swift, too unexpected, too volcanic. For a few moments his will power deserted him utterly, and he followed his breathless guide, or was dragged by her, through an open swing door and up a flight of stairs. Then they paused, at the top of the flight, and stood staring at each other.

Her dress was disarranged. He did not notice it— his eyes were too intent upon her face—until she drew his attention to it by hastily adjusting it. Probably the original Nell Gwynn played similar little tricks on the original Charles II, and probably Charles fell for them with even greater ease, protected from his sins by the strange prerogative of monarchs.

"I'm frightened!" she murmured.

So was James Shannon. This was not in the least what he had expected, or what he told himself he had expected. A few friendly words, a composed smile, perhaps a handshake . . . but, instead, this startling, pulsating moment, charged with high tension and drama! Things didn't happen like this. Not, at least, outside the bounds of private visions. But this was happening—or so he supposed!

"What's—what's the matter?" he heard himself saying.

"You saw the start of it."

"You mean——"

"Didn't you? When I was passing your box a little while ago—when I glanced at you?"

Her voice was still low and breathless, and she continually darted her eyes toward the stairs up which they had come.

"Yes, yes, I saw," he nodded.

Suddenly and disconcertingly, she switched away from narrative to the personal equation. The transition was so definite and impulsive—and so deft—that it carried him further into the emotional maelstrom in which he was floundering. "Tell me—I'm right? That *was* why you came? To help me?"

"Well, I—I admit I thought——"

"Don't say any more. I understand. It was funny, but somehow I'm not surprised—I knew you would." A tiny, half-wistful smile leaped into her eyes for a moment, then leaped away again like a fawn startled out of its play. "Let's find somewhere else! This is too near where I last shook him off. Then I'll tell you."

"Yes, but where?" he asked, as she seized his arm again.

Something began to rebel in him. It was not his sense of honor. It was his sense of dignity. Of male authority. Mr. Shannon, like many a starved sensualist, was a force in other spheres, and if his dominance did not shine very graciously in his own home, that

was merely because he was too close there to a gnaw-
ing realization of personal failure. Each member of
his family accused, unconsciously, his private
thoughts. Well, he had grown used to that, and he
accepted his sanctioned irritability as the only firm
route through the psychological morass. But at the
office, at the factory, there it was a very different story.
He was a force, a man who counted, a man who
decided and controlled. How could he have built up
his big business otherwise—the business, he constantly
told himself, on which his family depended for all
they had—and how, otherwise, could he be on the
road to a knighthood which would turn his wife into
Lady Shannon and his daughter into the worthy wife
of a rising M.P.? Private morality did not worry him
in his expensive office chair. Business morality ruled.
Business morality was direct and simple. All you had
to do was to be strong, walk forward, shove other
people out of your way, and help your country.

But the top of a staircase at the Chelsea Arts Ball
is neither one's home nor one's business, and when
one is standing there with a strange, attractive woman
a new code of morality has to be evolved. Exactly
what that code was, Mr. Shannon did not yet know,
but whatever it was, and wherever it led, he did not
think it should be entirely dissociated from male initiative. And this was why he now paused, momen-

tarily checking the fast-flowing tide with the question, "Yes—but where?"

"Anywhere! Does it matter?" she answered. And then, reading him, added, "Anywhere you like!"

The choice was made over to him, and proved an embarrassing gift. His knowledge of the Albert Hall was negligible. In fact, he could only recall having been in it once before, when he had watched Carnera knock some other boxer about, and then it had looked very different. Well, he had made his insignificant gesture. He presented the gift back again.

"It's all the same to me," he muttered. "You lead."

He regretted his choice of words. They rather gave him the sense of being a lamb. Again Nell Gwynn read him. It had to be a willing lamb.

"No, I've no right—this isn't fair," she murmured. "I'm presuming. Go back to your box."

It was another command, as she had meant it to be. Her choice of words was more astute than his.

"Nonsense, nonsense!" he replied. "Nothing of the sort! I'll see this through!"

Now he was properly committed!

With a sigh of relief, a very feminine sigh that flattered masculine strength, she turned and began walking. Finding himself behind, he hastened beside her, to rid himself of the sense of being a lamb. They walked quickly along a passage, a replica of the corridor below; then, after a moment's hesitation, she slipped to another staircase. In a very little while he had lost his bearings utterly.

"Have you any idea where we are?" he inquired presently.

"Not the slightest," she lied. She knew exactly where they were. In the vicinity of the great organ.

"Well—how about stopping here?" he suggested. He was a little breathless, though not entirely from physical exertion. "I expect we've—er—shaken him off?"

"I hope so!" she answered.

"We must have walked three miles!" He wanted to lighten the heavy atmosphere. There was something rather frightening about it. It had the sinister fascination of too much scent. He became suddenly conscious of the fact that his companion had too much scent. "Aren't there any chairs anywhere?"

"Perhaps, in there?" she suggested, pointing.

They were a few yards from the end of the corridor, and until she had pointed he had imagined they had reached a blind alley, but now he saw a narrow turn. It was ill-lit, and gave the impression of being out of bounds.

"Are we supposed to go in there?" he asked, like a schoolboy.

"So much the better if we're not!" she replied. "Then he won't be so likely to follow!"

A little laugh froze on her lips. Something had startled her. Genuinely this time. She seized Mr. Shannon's hand and lugged him forward. They passed into narrowness and shadows. Sudden darkness. Had they gone through a door? Mr. Shannon could not say. Now he tripped, as they turned round a dark corner with a descending step. She held him up.

"We'd better not go any farther!" he gasped.

"I agree," she whispered, to his relief. "I can see somewhere where we can sit."

"You've got better eyes than I have!"

"Just to the left. A sort of a ledge or step." She gave a little jump. For an instant he was alone in dark space. Then her voice came back to him through a gradually improving dimness. "I'm on!" she called. "Catch hold of my hand!"

She was only a foot or two off, after all. A white arm gleamed forward through the dimness. Assisted by it, he found a place beside her. He sat down rather limply.

"Yes, but where the devil are we?" he asked.

Again she lied, "I haven't the ghost!"

They were in a great, walled-off space that shut the big organ from the view of the hall. A dark, uneven cavern, evolved temporarily out of the need of the occasion. On their side of the enormous partition was silence and darkness. On the other side, brilliance and life. Yet this darkness was also brilliant, in its particular way. Brilliant with blinding, appalling possibilities.

The organ had played its last that night, and the organist had gone to bed.

Did any suspicion hover in Mr. Shannon's mind as he produced his overworked handkerchief and mopped his forehead? Had he been asked, he probably could not have answered. Perhaps there was a lurking doubt. Perhaps his racing thoughts may have wondered whether this bewildering, overscented woman was interested in him not merely as a means of escape from another human being, but as an escape also from the tragedy of boredom. But the situation was too inexplicable for the racing thoughts to work out, or to want to work out. For Mr. Shannon himself was trying to escape from the tragedy of boredom. Had his mind been steady and his blood cool when he had arrived at the hall, he would not have walked so obediently into this predicament.

"But what else could I have done?" he demanded of himself. That coherent thought did come to him as he mopped his brow, and as his companion sat silently beside him. "Each step—perfectly natural! No one can say I have forced or invited this! And—anyhow—is there anything to worry about?"

Breaking the silence, and anxious to explain it, he asked:

"Well—er—have you got your breath back?"

"Yes," she answered. "Have you?"

"I think so. I'm not so young as I was." There, that was a handsome admission! "It's been a bit of an obstacle race!"

"We're as young as we feel," she remarked. "I've got an idea 'you're not so very old."

"Well, I'm not a hundred," he conceded, temporizing. "But that's neither here nor there, is it? You're going to tell me how—how I can help you. That's the idea, isn't it?"

"You *have* helped me!" she replied. "You've taken me away from him!"

"I've taken you a little farther away from him," he pointed out, "but—does that complete the solution?"

"I don't know."

"You mean——? I'm still in the dark about the exact position."

"The exact position is that I'm safe for a while, and that's what I'm thanking you for." She added, with a little shiver which he felt against his arm, "Sufficient for the moment!"

"Safe," he repeated. "Well, of course you are! But you're not telling me that the fellow is actually *threatening* you?"

"Do you think I'd have gone to all this trouble—

and put *you* to all this trouble—if he hadn't been?" she retorted.

"I see. Yes. Of course," he murmured. "Drunk, I suppose?"

"What a lovely compliment!"

"Eh? I beg your pardon. Naturally, I wasn't implying—but *threats*! Hang it, a man doesn't threaten a woman unless he's drunk——"

"Or jealous?"

Mr. Shannon was silent.

"Oh, let's forget him for a few minutes!" she burst out. "For just five minutes. Will you? And then you shall go back, and I'll——"

"Yes, what will you do?" he asked, as she paused.

"Try and slip away quietly, and go home," she answered.

Her voice sounded depressed. Again he felt her arm against his own. "God, what a chance you've got!" shouted something crude inside him. "What the hell are you waiting for?"

"Yes, that might be best," he answered, sitting terribly still. "Yes—clearly—that will be best. Damn shame, though, spoiling your evening like this."

After a moment's silence came the reply, "I'm not complaining. You've given me something nice to remember."

Mr. Shannon continued to sit terribly still. She turned her head toward him in sudden anxiety. Wasn't he ever going to move? How much more would she have to do? She recalled the memorized page from his private diary, passed on to her by the spying employee who had found it while searching for other things. If the spy's own memory had been accurate, it had run like this: "Rather an odd interview with my doctor today. He couldn't find anything wrong with me to explain my condition, but just before I left he asked if I were happy with my wife, and when I asked him what he meant he said, 'People of our age, Mr. Shannon, are often quite happy with our wives, and go through a sort of physical hell in consequence.' 'Are you suggesting anything?' I asked. 'Not if there's nothing to suggest,' he answered. 'Apart from that you're as sound as a bell.' And feel as nervous as an old woman in a storm! Of course, the damn fool's right. But what is one to do about it? On my way back this evening tried on my Charles II suit for the Chelsea Arts Ball. . . ."

"I expect I'll remember it, too," said Mr. Shannon.

"God, he's putting up a fight!" thought Sally. "Is the silly old idiot going to beat me?" She knew that all she had to do was to lay her arm on his shoulder. She could not make out why she hesitated. "Hell! Here goes!"

Her arm slipped toward him through the dimness, but before it touched him she discovered herself on her feet.

"What's the matter?" he asked.

"I'm off!" she exclaimed fiercely.

She tried to pass him. He was between her and the
door through which they had come. But he caught
her skirt and held it.

"Why?" he demanded.

"Why, you poor baby?" she shot back. "Because
I shall kiss your innocent little face if I stay!"

"I see," said Mr. Shannon, very quietly, and still
holding on. "Well, why shouldn't you? Just once?"
He was amazed to find how momentarily calm he had
become, when actually on the verge of breathless experience. For it would be no less to Mr. Shannon.
"Let's talk it over."

"Talk it over?" she gasped hysterically. "You don't
talk things like this over! You do them, or you don't!"

"Then we won't talk it over," he answered.

She felt herself being pulled toward him. She felt
his arm go round her waist, preventing escape. For
the first time in her life she was weakened by self-
nausea.

"I *brought* you here for this!" she panted with lips
close to his.

"And then felt sorry for me and tried to run away
again," he whispered back. He was glad he had waited.
It was sweeter this way. "Don't feel sorry for me,
my dear. I want this more than you do."

Their lips pressed together.

And then came a blinding flash, and the tiny, metallic click of a little shutter. Mr. Shannon's strained arms grew limp, while the momentary gold in his heart became smeared with a horrible redness. For a second or two he could only see the redness.

The limp arms were empty. He heard her stumbling away, gasping and sobbing. He did not attempt to follow. That redness—it held him rooted.

Now she was gone. But still he sat, rooted. He knew that, although she had gone, he was not alone. Somebody remained; the somebody responsible for that flash and that click; and he had to regain his steadiness to deal with the somebody. Only by utter immobility, only by steeling himself against a frenzied desire to shriek and break things, could he hope to bring back balance to his tottering mind and strength to his weakened muscles.

The somebody was not far off. He was moving softly in a pool of blackness a little way below where Mr. Shannon sat. If he were making for the exit he would soon be nearer. Yes, now he was nearer, appearing suddenly like a dim shadow slipping by. "He doesn't know I'm still here," thought Mr. Shannon. "He believes I followed her out." The blinding flash had exaggerated the blackness of the immediately succeeding moments, and in those moments it would have been reasonable to assume that both had bolted. "But I have not bolted," thought Mr. Shannon. "I am still here."

He waited a few seconds longer. The shadow came closer still. Then, with an animal roar, Mr. Shannon leaped up and his fist shot out. The fist met air, and the force of it nearly wrenched his arm out of its socket; but the animal roar was more effective. The shadow gave a startled yelp, jumped back, stumbled, and fell. It fell, with a sickening thud, into the pit of blackness.

It did not rise again.

Mr. Shannon found himself out in the narrow passage. He did not know how he had got there. All he could recall was the sound of the thud, and then an attack of vertigo.

He leaned against the wall, breathing deeply and slowly. The air seemed fresh again. There was life in it. Light. From a distance came the faint sounds of music and laughter, like links with a forgotten past. "How wonderful existence would be," thought Mr. Shannon, "if only I could wipe out the last five minutes!" Through the new horror in his mind he could not understand how he had ever complained.

He became conscious that someone was approaching. Mechanically he felt for a cigarette, found one, and lit it. Then he walked out of the narrow passage into a broader one.

It soothed his shocked vanity to find that he was walking calmly and steadily. He could still function. He passed the person who had been approaching—a little man in loud slacks—without giving away his agitation. A faint hope stirred in his mind. Perhaps, after all, if he kept steady. . . .

Five minutes later he walked into his box.

"Hallo, Dad," exclaimed his wife, with a smile of welcome. "Did you enjoy your drink?"

Mr. Shannon did not know whether or not he had left a dead man in the little black hell from which he had escaped, but Mr. Warwick Hilling was in no state of doubt as he staggered out of the stifling sitting room and groped his way blindly through the misty passage. The little chauffeur whose mysterious instructions had led to this unbelievable situation, and whose pound notes were in Hilling's pocket at that moment, controlled him no longer. He was indubitably dead.

How had he died? From the effect of the scratch on his wrist? There were such things as poisoned arrows; were there such things as poisoned bullets? Or from his wine? Or from the heavily-laden atmosphere that

made one think of gas ovens? The air was foul and
sickly, and as Hilling had approached the dead man
his bursting lungs had been nearly stifled by a heavy,
stagnant cloud. . . . Once, in the war . . . yes, yes,
but for the time being, that did not matter. All that
mattered was to get out of this house of death—and to
find a policeman.

Previously a policeman had been merely a possible
solution. Now a policeman became the only solution.
In other words, Hilling had given up.

He found his way somehow to the front door. He
fumbled with the knob, for the heavily-laden atmosphere seemed to be following him and to be pressing
him against the wood. He was no longer dancing
politely with a chair, he was wrestling with a gas
oven. But he managed to get the door open before
the gas oven won, and to lurch out into the invisible
front garden.

He lurched onto the hard ground. It rose and hit
him long before he thought he had reached it. He
lay for a moment or two, partly to get his breath, and
partly to see whether it would hit him again.
Happily it did not, although any happiness the fact
may have brought was strictly temporary.

He rose. Fog walled all round him. He saw nothing
but walls of fog. It seemed impossible that, a few
yards from where he stood, there was a lighted room

with a dead man sitting in it. That he could turn round and, within a few seconds, return to that other world. This world was bad enough, but the world behind him, with its sickly, deathly silence broken only by the whispering of a little clock, was infinitely worse. He was glad that his immediate and obvious duty lay outside the house, even though he felt an odd sense of desertion while he began to creep away from it.

"I'll come back, old man," he thought muzzily. "I'll see someone pays for this! You're in England now, you know!"

He forgot, in his anxiety to grasp homely realities, that the little chauffeur was not in England, but in an uncharted region beyond the smallness of geographical barriers.

Ridiculous though his thoughts were, their comparative coherence disturbed him. His thoughts must not become too coherent just yet, he realized. The return to logic would focus his emotions, and the need of his emotions was to remain unformed; to lean. He would like to have cried on a woman's breast. Even on the dead chauffeur's breast. A terrible tenderness for the chauffeur was stealing over him, moving him dangerously.

Now he was at the gate. It surprised him, vaguely, to find that it was still there. It was open, just as he had left it. He paused before stepping out onto the pavement.

Then a figure loomed in the fog, paused also, and stood watching him. A large, bulky figure, without much outline.

"Hi!" gasped Hilling, in a cracked voice. "Policeman!"

The large figure stirred, but did not advance. That seemed to prove he was a policeman.

"Quick! In here! Murder!" cried Hilling.

This time the figure did advance. It leaped upon Hilling, encircled him with great arms, and bore him out of the yellowness into blackness.

Two A.M.

WHEN Henry Brown rose, as reported by Conrad Shannon from Box No. 12, and left the attractive nymph who was sitting beside him, he was obeying an instinct that had been steadily developing ever since the coster had knocked his champagne glass out of his hand and had stolen the queer-looking light from his pocket. The nymph had argued that the light might be the coster's own property. Henry agreed that this was very possibly true. But when you are regaining your own property you do not employ the methods of a pickpocket unless the property has some sinister implication.

Henry did not really believe in his startling theory that the torch was a bomb. He did believe, however, that the coster was "up to something," and that the torch *might* be a bomb, and his sudden evolution into the realms of manhood gave him an increased sense of responsibility. The most wonderful girl in the world—you could never have convinced Henry in his present mood that his companion was not the most

175

wonderful girl in the world—had expressed a good opinion of him. She had referred to his physical pluck, she was honoring him by dancing with him, and she had hinted, if vaguely, that one day they might win a dancing championship together. The only way to justify such a position was to prove oneself worthy of it in every department of one's being.

Adventure had caught the humble little fellow right off the ground, and he was living at the dizzy top of it. If he eventually fell and bumped his head, that was for the future.

It was ironic that the individual who caused him to speed from his seat was not the individual Henry thought he was, just as it was ironic that, when the nymph rose rather anxiously to follow, a shower of chocolates should shoot out at her from the parapet of Box No. 12 and delay the pursuit. In that delay she lost sight of her peripatetic companion, and was prevented from interfering with a journey that was destined to lead to a disconcerting conclusion.

Henry raced after his quarry. The quarry, whom he had spotted from a considerable way off, unconsciously led him the deuce of a distance. Henry darted, as it were, from glimpse to glimpse; out of the ballroom; back in the ballroom; out again; along a length of corridor; up a flight of stairs; into a cloakroom; out of the cloakroom; along another length of corridor.

And when at last he bumped breathlessly into his quarry's back, he discovered his mistake. He had certainly chased a coster, but it was not the right coster. "Hal-*lo*!" exclaimed the wrong coster. "What's the excitement?"

"My mistake!" stammered Henry, panting.

"And my back," said the wrong coster.

"I thought you were somebody else," explained Henry.

"Do it again and you'll wish *you* were!" retorted the wrong coster. "You hit me bang in the middle of my lumbago!"

They parted—but not forever. They were to meet again under even less happy conditions.

While Henry regained his breath he saw a girl somewhere out of the corner of his eye, but he did not realize it until he had returned to the ballroom and had found that the nymph was missing. "Of course she's looking for me," he reflected. She was. And then he remembered the girl he had seen out of the corner of his eye, and hastened back to the spot. But naturally, she was not there. Even if she had been, he would have found her as disappointing as the wrong coster.

A terrible despair began to settle upon him. Suppose he did not find her? Suppose he never found her? Suppose he never saw her again? The idea was not supportable. What a fool he had been not to get her name—yes, and her address. . . .

He wandered about, like a lost dog, searching without a plan. He found himself in a part of the hall he had not been in before. It was a blind alley. At least he thought it was. He turned, and began to retrace his steps. He went round a corner, and suddenly paused and turned again. He thought he heard footsteps from the direction of the blind alley.

A couple of strides brought him back to the point from where he could see the blind alley. A head was peering cautiously from a dark strip of shadow. Evidently there was a small passage there or something. The head abruptly vanished. It had remained visible for barely a second, but in that second Henry believed he had identified it. The coster . . . and the right one this time. . . .

Now Henry himself popped back as he heard more footsteps coming along the corridor from the opposite direction. The direction from which he himself had come before he had turned back and gone round this corner. Without knowing exactly why, he remained concealed till the newcomers passed the opening in which he stood. Perhaps he remained concealed because he felt something queer in the atmosphere. But he did not know exactly why there was anything queer in the atmosphere, either. Although, of course, if he had not made a second mistake, and if that head *had* been the head of the right coster, the theory that he was "up to something" gained color.

The newcomers went by. They did not see Henry. They were too absorbed in themselves. But Henry saw them distinctly. One of them was a very attractive woman, highly scented—he caught the whiff of her scent as she passed—and in what he described generally as "one of those historical costumes." The man with her was also wearing an historical costume. It was the man he had noticed, and had once stared at, in Box No. 12.

He waited for them to turn and come back. As they did not come back he grew curious, and advanced a step or two. Now he could see them again. They were standing by the dark shadow from which the coster's head had appeared. Straining forward, he lost his balance and tripped. The woman raised her head suddenly, and, without turning, quickly vanished into the dark shadow with her companion.

Now they were gone, and Henry was alone once more.

"Funny!" he thought. "Or—isn't it? Am *I* funny?"

He could not decide. He felt nervous and dissatisfied with himself. He wondered whether, if the last two people had not come along, he would have gone through that dark narrow passage himself to interview the coster? He wondered what, had he done so, would have happened.

"But, of course, I can't go poking my nose in there now, can I?" he asked himself. "Well, I mean to say—can I?"

He began to walk away. The sense of personal dissatisfaction increased. Was he making excuses to himself? Was he funking something, even while he did not know what it was he funked? His mind felt confused. He thought again of the friendly beef-eater with the long nose. Then he thought of his lost nymph, and of the story he would have to tell her if he found her. "Wherever have you been?" "Chasing that chap who took the torch out of my pocket." "Did you find him?" "Yes." "What happened?" "Nothing!" "Why not?" "Well, you see, I came away again——"

He paused when the imaginary conversation reached this point. It did not sound particularly impressive. Hardly the sort of conversation calculated to keep him in her good opinion. And he wanted to remain in her good opinion, as also in the good opinion of himself. He remodeled the imaginary conversation: "Wherever have you been?" "Chasing that confounded bloke who took the torch out of my pocket." "Did you find him?" "You bet I found him!" "What happened?" "Well, I'll tell you. I saw his head for a moment in a dark passage. It popped away almost at once, but I was after it! I went into the dark passage, and then——"

Yes—and then?

He would have to find out. No alternative existed that could uphold his new dignity! He would have to complete his story, and his emancipation!

So he turned—he had turned more times in the last ten minutes than Dick Whittington—and as he turned someone came blundering toward him. It was the historical lady who had disappeared into the dark passage with the historical man, after the coster. She did not stop, or even pause, and while she went by him Henry had an uncanny feeling that she did not see him. Her eyes looked dazed and seemed to be staring blindly above her flushed cheeks.

"That's queer!" he muttered.

He stared after her. He toyed with the idea of questioning her. What about catching up with her and asking her if she had happened to see a chap dressed like a coster? But now she was out of sight—and perhaps it hadn't been much of an idea, anyway.

He continued his halting progress toward the dark passage. He was fighting nasty premonitions. Hallo! What was that? He thought he heard something. Once more he stopped.

"Get a move on!" he told himself. "You're worse than a bus!"

Now he saw the shadow that marked the dark passage. He had reached the spot from where he had made his previous observations. Halt, again! Somebody was coming out of the passage. Swaying out, as though he were drunk. . . .

The historical man, this time. His eyes didn't seem to be seeing any more than the eyes of the historical lady. He was leaning against a wall.

But as Henry advanced he moved abruptly, and groped toward his pocket. For an instant Henry thought of revolvers, which showed the condition of his mind, but all the historical man brought out was a cigarette case. Quickly but coolly the historical man lit a cigarette, and walked toward Henry as he slipped the case back into his pocket. He passed Henry quietly, without a sign or a tremor.

"That's *queerer*!" thought Henry. "He didn't look as cool as that when he first came out of the passage!"

Well, three people had gone in, and two had come out again. The third person was still there, and it was the third person he had to interview.

Now Henry was in the dark, narrow passage. He wanted to linger, as he had lingered when leaving his bedroom to come to the ball. He felt again that he was saying good-by to himself, or to some established

order of things appertaining to himself. The same
Henry Brown would never re-enter that bedroom!
Would the same Henry Brown emerge from this
passage?

He came to a doorway. The door was open. Beyond was dimness. What sort of a place was he coming
to? There didn't seem to be any rhyme or reason in
it. There were steps at unexpected places. You had
to be careful not to trip. Was it a sort of vast store-
room for odds and ends? Or a disused warehouse?
Don't be silly, how could it be a warehouse? Or was
it the place where they had kept the stunts? . . .

His foot kicked something. A small object that
clattered away as he kicked it. He followed the direction of the clatter, nearly stumbled down a single
step, stooped, and picked up the object.

"Well, I'm blowed!" he murmured. "Camera!"

The next moment he forgot the camera. Unconsciously he slipped it into one of his capacious pockets,
with the instinctive desire to retain possession of it
and to have both hands free. His foot had now
touched another object, and this other object was
larger, and did not clatter away from him. It was
also softer.

Henry stooped again. His heart almost stopped
beating. He knew, before he touched it, that he was
stooping over the body of a man. The man's costume

winked up at him, gleaming incongruously through
the darkness. It was a spiritual darkness. . . .

"Here! What's the matter?" said Henry.

At least he intended to say it, but afterward he
believed that he had only thought the words loudly.
His throat was temporarily out of action.

Even if he had spoken the words he would have
received no answer.

Two visions came hurtling through his mind, like
vivid nightmares. One was of the historical woman
who had passed him with unseeing eyes. The other
was of the historical gentleman who had come swaying out of this place, had leaned against the wall, and
had then abruptly recovered himself, lit a cigarette,
and coolly walked away.

The second vision, unpleasant though it was, had
one useful result. It reminded Henry of the soothing
qualities of nicotine. Emulating the historical gentleman, he lit a cigarette. Then he counted twelve puffs.
Then he walked out of the black hell into the corridor. If it was not a different Henry Brown who
emerged from the passage, it was one who had touched
grim tragedy for the first time in his life. The Albert
Hall was giving him his first experiences of both the
depths and the heights. . . .

In a corridor he met a Chinaman.

"Ah! You're the very person I've been looking for!" exclaimed the Chinaman. "Please, a light!"

Henry was amazed at the steadiness of his hand as he took his cigarette from his mouth and held it toward the unlighted cigarette of the Chinaman.

"Thank you," smiled the Chinaman, and glanced casually at the camera sticking out of Henry's bulging pocket. "Have you taken some good photographs?"

"What about a drink, sir?" asked Harold Lankester, and added in a lower tone, "I'd rather like a word with you."

Mr. Shannon sat very still for a moment. "Does he know anything?" he thought. "Nonsense—how can he?" Then he answered:

"Certainly. But—er—how about Dorothy?"

"She's going to dance the next one with Conrad," interposed Mrs. Shannon, "and I'm sitting out!"

"Good-by my toes!" murmured Dorothy.

"First prize for rudeness," retorted Conrad.

The two men rose. Mr. Shannon walked slowly to the door of the box, but his mind moved more rapidly.

"He can't know," he thought. "It's impossible. But, even if he does know, there's nothing to do about it. My position is perfectly simple. I have been foolish—yes, but that's all. Anybody can be foolish, and the average fool would have gone a damn sight further than I did. By God, yes! As for the man, well, I just knocked him down, as he deserved, and now he's probably nursing a bump." Mr. Shannon would have given more than a hundred pounds to have been sure that the man was nursing a bump. The fellow had lain horribly still. But even the happier alternative had its desperate side. "Why the devil didn't I keep my head?" he thought. "Why didn't I get hold of that camera before I left him? I'd have gone back if I hadn't met that confounded little fellow in the check slacks. He's everywhere, that chap. I wonder if he is a member of the gang?" His soul groaned. He tried to wrench his mind back to the immediate moment. "Harold. Now, then, what's this he's going to talk to me about?"

They had left the box and were walking toward a bar. An idea suddenly occurred to Mr. Shannon, and his companion, watching him silently, noted the little pink flush that leaped into his cheek, but did not interpret it.

"Why, of course," Mr. Shannon was thinking. "It's about Dorothy!"

But it was not about Dorothy, as he learned a couple of minutes later when they sat on a couch with their glasses in their hands.

"I hope you won't misunderstand what I'm going to say, sir," began Lankester.

"Eh?" jerked Mr. Shannon, his heart suddenly sinking again.

This was not a very propitious start.

"As a matter of fact, it's not going to be too easy," continued Lankester, looking at his nails. "But when knowledge happens to come your way——"

"Oh! You know something!" interrupted Mr. Shannon, nervously.

"Yes."

"H'm. Well—be sure of your ground, my boy."

"Unfortunately—in one sense, unfortunately—I am quite sure of my ground. The facts are indisputable, or I——"

"Wait a moment!" Mr. Shannon's voice was tense. Harold Lankester looked at him curiously. "Facts, yes. But how about the interpretation of those facts? That's—that's where so many of you politicians go wrong—and where we businessmen are ahead of you. We judge what's behind the fact, and avoid wrong conclusions!"

Mr. Shannon took out his hard-worked handkerchief and wiped his forehead. His handkerchief and his forehead had never before met so often in a single evening. He felt he was floundering, saying weak, foolish things, but he could not bear to listen to the words he believed were on Lankester's lips. The humiliation would be unendurable! Already there was something in Lankester's expression. . . .

"Nevertheless, sir, I'm going to risk it," said Lankester, "and you can accept the warning or not."

"Warning," repeated Mr. Shannon dully. "Well?"

"You know," said Lankester, "that I've been attending conferences on the Near East situation?"

Mr. Shannon sat very still. Relief surged through him with a sweetness that was almost nauseating. He really felt a little sick.

"Near East," he murmured thickly. "Go on."

"You can guess what's coming?" inquired Lankester.

In his reaction Mr. Shannon indulged in a feeble little joke with himself.

"Never guess when you're going to be told," he answered. "What's up with the Near East?"

"Isn't something always up with the Near East?"

Mr. Shannon nodded while Lankester continued:

"It's where you go to when you want to buy a war. But sometimes it's easier to buy a war than at other times. Everything's set. Political situation—emotional situation—military situation——" He paused. "Even down to the mathematics of the munition supplies."

Mr. Shannon looked at him sharply. His business instinct suddenly flared. For a moment there was no

such person as Nell Gwynn, or as a blackmailing photographer paying too heavily, perhaps, for his sins.
The Albert Hall dissolved, and in its stead was an
office, with a factory hard by.

"So *that's* it, is it?" muttered Mr. Shannon.

"Ah, now you *do* guess," came Lankester's quiet
voice.

"And maybe you don't!" retorted Mr. Shannon.
"I suppose you think you're the first?"

"First what?"

"To try and queer this big deal! I've been badgered
for weeks. Not openly, of course. Quietly, privately.
First, just requests. As if we broke our contracts to
please any Tom, Dick or Harry! Then, bribery. Why,
even if I accepted bribes, they couldn't name a figure
that would make it worth my while!"

It was on the tip of Lankester's tongue to ask
whether Mr. Shannon had gone into the figure, but
he desisted.

"And after that, interference! You know we've
had trouble? I've had to discharge some of my people
for prying and spying—and worse. We were on the
edge of a bad strike! And now——"

He stopped abruptly. He had said more than he
meant to. Confound this lack of control!

"Who *were* the Tom, Dick and Harry?" inquired
Lankester.

"I think I'll keep that to myself," replied Mr. Shannon. "If you don't mind."

"Not at all, sir," answered Lankester. "You see, I'm afraid it won't make any difference, either way. The natural- supposition, of course, is that the Tom, Dick and Harry were the people against whom your munitions were to be used——"

"Whoa! Not so fast!" muttered Mr. Shannon, although Lankester's voice had been kept low. He glanced up and down the corridor. Nobody was interested. "This is a—a private order."

"From a man with a rather large estate!"

"I don't measure my customers' estates!"

"Or count the number of pigeons your guns will bring down?"

"That's not my business!"

There was a short silence. A man and a girl suddenly chased toward them. The man made a snatch at the girl, she ducked, and stumbled into Mr. Shannon's lap. "Hallo, someone's got the luck!" guffawed the man. The girl shrieked, leaped up again, and vanished, the man after her.

"No, sir, technically speaking, it's not your business," said Lankester, "which is why, politically speaking, it sometimes has to be another person's business."

"Are *you* the other person?" demanded Mr. Shannon. As Lankester did not reply, he added, "Well, then, I'll wait till the other person comes along—and if he doesn't come along for a couple of days, I won't worry."

Lankester waited an instant. He was battling against a sensation of nausea. He did not exaggerate Mr. Shannon's attitude, or blame him especially for his self-interest. He knew that it was the common attitude, and in his own walk of life he saw it reflected on all sides. But moments came when he found himself fighting a sickening hopelessness, when he wanted to scrap all the careful rules and wise controls on which he had built his life. And then he waited, till the dangerous impulse was over.

"It's coming along tomorrow," he said.

Mr. Shannon wheeled round.

"Tomorrow?" he exclaimed. And then repeated more softly, "Tomorrow?"

"Of course, only in the form of a request—at first. But I assure you, sir, it'll save the hell of a lot of trouble if you agree to the request."

"Oh! And *I* get no trouble for breaking a contract?"

"I think I can guarantee that."

"And I lose nothing?"

"There may be an alternative market nearer home—perhaps yielding a little less money, but providing more certainty of getting it."

Mr. Shannon looked thoughtful. He had no per-

sonal interest in the customer with the large estate . . .
or in the pigeons that might be shot. Once you started
thinking along those lines, you'd just sit in a chair
and twiddle your thumbs, and the world would stop.
Do your job, and let others do theirs. . . .

"What's the position?" demanded Mr. Shannon suddenly.

"It might be something like this," answered Lankester. "I'll suggest it alphabetically. The constitution
of a country called A is being threatened by another
country called B. When B has received certain munitions from a firm in C—not before—one of its lesser
statesmen will be shot at by a paid fanatic in A. This
will give B an excuse for invading A. An old for-
mula, but invariably effective."

"No, not invariably," interrupted Mr. Shannon.

"You're right," retracted Lankester. "Generally—
not invariably. But B's chances of success are always
increased if some larger country—Z—is fathering the
enterprise for separate reasons of its own. Z may even
finance it. B may want the little war, but Z may
want a big war. It may be just the moment for Z.
But not, Mr. Shannon," added Lankester, "for X. In
fact X may dislike war intensely on any account."

"I see," murmured Mr. Shannon, seeing perfectly.
"Of course, you know there is a clause that says,
'Time is the essence of the contract.'"

"Of course," nodded Lankester, rather dryly. "In this case it is particularly the essence. If you are a week late, as it happens, your munitions will be of no use to B."

"Why not?"

"Because, in a week's time, A would be prepared for the sudden attack, and could meet it."

"And attack herself?"

"No. B is the aggressor—this time. A wants peace. So you see, Mr. Shannon, if B cannot attack speedily and successfully—in other words, *this* week—there will be no attack. There will be no war. And the larger country I have designated as X will be delighted."

"H'm," grunted Mr. Shannon. "It's a pity this country you call X couldn't have made up its mind a bit sooner!"

"I agree," answered Lankester sincerely. "As a matter of fact, when peaceful A discovered the plot, they approached us——"

"Us?"

"I should say, X," Lankester corrected himself, with a smile. "But as X was not entirely sympathetic at that moment, and her general policy was vague and undecided, the peaceful A evidently determined not to wait, and——"

"Approached me direct."

"So I understand."

"Yes, and when *I* wasn't entirely sympathetic, the peaceful A tried underhand methods—for which, as far as I'm concerned, they could be blown to smithereens!"

"Yes, but not as far as X is concerned."

"I see. I've *got* to submit, then?"

"There is no compulsion whatever. You and I are just talking things over unofficially——"

"Oh, to hell with your politics!" burst out Mr. Shannon. "I'm sorry, my boy, but all this shillyshally-ing . . . I like blunt dealings!"

Harold Lankester studied the carpet.

"You can have them," he said.

"Well, we'd know where we were! As it is, I'm to do something X wants, but X won't take the respon-sibility! So what am I to tell my client?"

"You mentioned just now that time was the essence of the contract."

"Certainly."

"Then if you are behind your time, through some unavoidable delay—machinery, strike, anything—you can't deliver, and the contract lapses."

"You've worked it all out, I see," observed Mr. Shannon. "But suppose there's a penalty clause? Have you worked *that* out?"

"Yes, I've even worked that out," answered Lan-kester, "but unofficially, this time. I have no author-ity whatever for reminding you of a cynical remark I once heard: 'A country honors its dead, and gives

honors to its living.' Of course, each kind of honor
has its price."

Then Lankester rose rather abruptly and walked
away.

Mr. Shannon looked after him, his mind grappling
with this new confusion. Oddly, it was not the contract itself he was worrying about. From the hints
that had been dropped, that matter would straighten
itself out, and in the end might prove to his advantage. . . . " 'A country honors its dead, and gives
honors to its living.' " . . . But there had been something disturbing in Harold's manner. Something not
entirely complimentary. "Say what you like," reflected
Mr. Shannon lugubriously, "once you begin to develop
an inferiority complex, it's the devil to get rid of
again!"

He waited for a minute or two. Then he rose and
walked back to his box, while an amorous couple who
had been eying the couch with furtive longing made
a hasty dart for it, and discussed matters of less public importance.

Outside the box he met his son, coming from the
other direction.

"Aren't you dancing with Dorothy?" asked Mr.
Shannon.

"I was," replied Conrad, "but I have yielded her
to a Balkan Prince."

"The devil you have!" exclaimed Mr. Shannon.

"Ah, not a real Balkan Prince, Dad," explained Conrad. "Merely an actor."

"Well, I can't say I think it was wise," frowned Mr. Shannon.

"Nor do I," answered Conrad sadly, "and it didn't do any good, either."

"What's that mean?"

Conrad shook his head, and looked sadder than ever. His father poked his head forward and regarded him closely.

"Have you been drinking?" he demanded.

"I did have one stiff soda," said Conrad, and then suddenly giggled. "Sorry, Dad, but this idiotic place knocks all the sense out of you. Course I was a mad hat to give Dorothy up, but do you know why I did it? I wanted to chance my own luck with Nell Gwynn. Have you seen her?" He grinned, but his father's expression chased the grin away. Whew! What was the matter with him? Dash it all, on a ridiculous night like this, couldn't one ask. . . . "Anyway, I *didn't* have any luck," he concluded lamely. "So I've come along to trip it with the mater."

Sally was certainly in no mood for dancing. After her tumultuous exit from the unsavory chamber of darkness in which she had trapped her elderly victim, and regretted it too late, she had waited for Sam in the spot arranged and had waited in vain. Then she had returned to the unsavory chamber of darkness, had poked her head through the narrow passage, and had called Sam's name softly. Receiving no response she had concluded he was not there. There seemed no reason why he should still be there, nor was there any reason why, if he had been there, he should not have answered. So, having no relish for a wild goose chase, she had turned her back on the place, and tried her luck in the body of the hall.

"Sam's a fool, if ever there was one!" she fretted. "Yes—and so am I!"

For what was she going to do when she found Sam and received the camera from him? Pass it on—or destroy it?

While descending the final flight of stairs she suddenly paused. A wretched thought had struck her to explain Sam's absence. Perhaps he had missed her on purpose! Perhaps he meant to pass the camera on himself, and for his own figure!

The next instant she was calling herself an idiot. He *could* not pass it on. He did not know whom to pass it on to. She had carefully withheld that knowledge from him. . . .

Reaching the ballroom, she paused again. Two men had been in her thoughts, and now she all but ran into one of them. The Balkan Prince was standing on the outer circle of the dancers, and his head was moving slowly, as though following the course of one of the couples. Sally tried to pick out the couple, but failed to do so—for it was difficult to judge the exact direction of the Prince's eyes by the back of his head—until the couple had reached the nearest point of their orbit; and then she only identified them because they stopped.

She recognized the couple as Mr. Shannon's son and daughter.

After that, surprising things happened. The Prince took a step forward. Mr. Shannon's daughter seemed anxious to continue dancing, but Mr. Shannon's son did not. He was staring, not at the Prince, but at Sally herself.

"What's that mean?" Sally wondered.

The meaning soon became clear. The Prince took another step forward and asked, in a low undertone:

"Would Madame du Barry honor a humble prince?"

Madame du Barry looked confused, and her attempt at indignation was not too successful. The Prince's accent was rather charming.

"Someone's spotted who you are!" exclaimed her brother with a grin. "He deserves a prize for his smartness!"

"You permit me to usurp her, then, for just a few minutes—if she herself is willing?" murmured the Prince.

"She didn't say she was willing," retorted Madame du Barry, suddenly finding her voice.

"Oh, come, Sis, be a sport!" remonstrated her brother. "Chelsea comes but once a year, and therefore let's be merry!"

But the Prince shook his head.

"The humble Prince apologizes to Madame du Barry," he said. "Pardon him for a foolish hope."

Then Madame du Barry capitulated, though whether through inclination or embarrassment Sally could not tell. Nor was she given long for conjecture, for the Balkan Prince had hardly glided with his partner into the tide before the partnerless youth bounced upon her. "And now would Nell Gwynn honor a humble God-knows-what?" he cried.

"No, thank you," answered Sally definitely.

The face of the God-knows-what fell. He had not expected this defeat, for there are. moods in which rebuff seems impossible. Lacking the advantages of Balkan tact and splendor—for a golden statue may be dazzling, but it is not necessarily impressive—this golden statue came down with a bump.

"Oh, I say!" was its ineffective comment.

"You see, I'm not dancing," explained Sally, responding to a vague sensation of sympathy.

"That's not the reason," gloomed the disappointed one.

"If I gave you the real reason, young man," thought

Sally, "you'd get a shock!" The real reason was that she was looking for a man who had photographed the boy's father while kissing her! Aloud she said, "What makes you say that?"

"Because I've *seen* you dancing," answered the boy. "I'll tell you who with. That chap all over pearl buttons."

"But I'm not dancing any more—with him or anybody. By the way, have you seen him anywhere about lately?" she added suddenly.

"What! Have you lost him?"

She nodded.

"What do I get if I find him?" he asked. "A fox trot?"

She hesitated. He was a nuisance, but he might prove useful.

"Perhaps," she compromised.

"Good, I'll hold you to it," he exclaimed. "But first I will go and finish this dance with my mother. She has been rather neglected, and I am one of those saintly little boys who die young. A short life and not even a merry one. Heigh-ho!"

He would have been surprised had he known of the odd expression that followed him as he sped away.

Warwick Hilling opened his eyes in a smoke-filled room. There were other things in the room, but the smoke was all his consciousness first returned to. It wreathed through the darkness, it made his eyes smart. Then he noticed that it appeared to be coming from two quarters, and that every now and then a tiny glow, like the light of a miniature volcano, came and went, illuminating for a meager instant indecipherable outlines.

Soon it occurred to him that he himself was a more important matter to notice than the smoke. He was, he concluded after a few moments of doubt, complete. Portions of his anatomy seemed very far away, and it was this sense of distance that had contributed to his original doubts. "But I am not well," he told himself, to soothe an oppressed vanity, "and when you are not well, space as well as time gets mixed up."

He recalled—deliberately, for he preferred for a little while to dwell on the past than to try to probe the present—he recalled an attack of indigestion he had once had. Somewhere in Asia. He could not remember the exact country. He had eaten something native, purely in compliment to his host, and three hours later it had transformed the entire universe into a series of expanding circles. Small circles that augmented into vast circles, and that carried his limbs away with them on their vanishing horizons. He had been lying down then, in bed. Now, also, he was lying down. But he could not be in Asia. No, that was impossible. Where was he then? The past receded, and the present remained. He would have to probe the present, if only to alter it.

"Ah, I have it!" he thought. "This is my Houdini Act!"

His Houdini Act was the least glorious of his achievements, and he resorted to it only when all else failed and the cupboard was empty. Its one bright spot was the girl who had to superintend the binding, and see that it was not too tight. She had to be a pretty girl, of course—it was the demand of the public—but Hilling always understood the public attitude when her fingers played over the ropes or lightly touched his face.

"Yes, but she's messed it up this time," decided Hilling, "because the ropes are so tight I can't move. . . . Or have I forgotten the old trick? My God, suppose I've forgotten!"

He strained his limbs. The cords cut into them. Ah, of course, now he remembered. One began at the wrist—the secret was at the wrist. He worked his hands quietly, subtly. They remained bound.

Perspiration that he could not reach rose to the forehead of Warwick Hilling.

The present no longer had to be probed. It bore down upon him, reaching him with the sudden force of an express train. This was not his Houdini Act.

No pretty girl stood within a few paces of his head, with her hands clasped and an anxious yet confident smile. He was in a dark, smoke-fouled chamber, somewhere in the heart of London. At least, he supposed that. And not very far off a little foreigner lay dead—"Good, so?" came his voice ironically through the black tunnel of memory—and people were dancing in the Albert Hall. . . .

One of the little glows broke the darkness, and a low mutter came from behind it. Another mutter responded. Hilling was fully conscious now, and he found the consciousness painful.

"I think it would do me good," he reflected, "to say something violent."

He made the attempt, but failed. He found that he could not manipulate his mouth.

But in a few moments a dim form bent over him, and after two small eyes had been lowered near to his, two hands advanced toward his face and removed the gag.

"Not dead—still alife," came the voice of the doubtful Samaritan.

"Yes, sir, I am still alive," spluttered Hilling, "but the credit is mine, not yours—ah!"

The exclamation was caused by a cloud of smoke that was puffed rudely into his face. When it had cleared the faintly seen face had withdrawn, but the voice came again from a little distance.

"You spik what you are ask, no more, and you spik low. You un'stan', so?"

Oddly, it was the final word that affected Hilling the most. It reminded him of another who had used it—another whose accent had been similar, but so much more attractive. While he fought his emotion, the voice sounded again, but now in its own tongue, and it was directed softly to the other person in the room.

The incomprehensible muttering continued for a little. Then the original speaker reverted to broken English, and addressed Hilling again.

"Now, please, to begin. Who are you?"

"Why should I tell you who I am?" replied Hilling, with all the dignity that could be mustered from a recumbent position.

"Becoss I ask."

"And why should I do what you ask?"

The inquiry seemed to amuse his audience. Then came the reason. It pressed suddenly into his chest.

"I show you! You feel, so? And there is other. The gas. You know that, too, I think."

The revolver pressed harder in his chest. "A hero dies but once!" Hilling repeated to himself. He was not quite certain, however, whether he deserved the title, for after he had died the revolver was withdrawn.

"Now, spik," said his aggressor. "Two time I ask, who are you? Three time, no. Un'stan'?"

"My name is Warwick Hilling," replied Hilling.

"Who is Warwick Hilling?"

"A man of culture would not have to ask that question, sir! I am an actor, of some repute——"

"Ahi! Actor! And is it a part, so? The clothes?"

A murmur came from the second man, but the first man shut him up.

"Spik quick! It is not to wait! The clothes, explain it, or here is the finish!"

The revolver made a little glint again as it was raised to a threatening position. Hilling swallowed and replied:

"I am permitted, perhaps, to go to a fancy dress ball?"

"Ahi! A ball?"

"I believe I said so."

"And that is why you wear this clothes?"

"I do not generally go about in this costume."

"No! That is so! You wear the stiff collar to choke. But you can be choke as you are, so spik and say why this clothes——"

"I have told you——"

"Wait till I finish, wait till I finish! Pig! *This* clothes, I say, and not another? To fool us, so? Ahi! But now you see who it is the fool!"

Anger spat from the voice. Then it grew calm

again. He was like a bad edition of the first, the happier foreigner Hilling had met that evening.

Hilling's mind began to race. Since silence was denied him by the revolver, he must invent some story, for it was obvious that these two murderous fellows must not learn that he had exchanged places with the Prince. That would reveal the Prince's whereabouts. . . .

A sharp oath rang out.

"How much longer! One, two, three more, and I kill you! Bang, finish! Now, spik quick. Why this clothes, and why were you in—that house?"

"I will explain," replied Hilling slowly. He spoke slowly, so that his chaotic mind might have a chance of keeping pace with his words. "It was a—a sheer coincidence. I had selected this costume because—having performed many times in the East—before Crowned Heads, you may be interested to know—I have always felt that this was a form of raiment I could carry. It suited my figure—my atmosphere——"

"Yes, yes, but not so many words!" came the impatient interruption.

"You have asked me a question, and I am answering it!" replied Hilling stiffly.

It was easy to act stiffly, since he had never felt stiffer.

"But you answer all night!" cried the other. "And

now you say the costume is one you like. So, so! And that is why you choose it to go to the ball. So, so! But you do not go to the ball. You go, instead, to that house."

"You wish to know why?" inquired Hilling searching for a reason.

"I insist to know why!" exclaimed the enemy.

"And then, when I am telling you, you interrupt me," retorted Hilling, still searching for a reason. "I believe you called me a pig, sir. A pig, at least, has some brains."

For an instant Hilling thought his last moment had come. Possibly a mutter from the second foreigner saved him. The first quietened down sufficiently to hiss:

"Say why, *quick*!"

"Because, sir, I was sent for."

"Oh!"

"Yes, sir—sent for!" And, as he floundered, a solution suddenly flashed into his tired mind. He continued with more confidence. "It was, after all, understandable. You see, my photograph had appeared in the papers—before the ball, you understand. Famous people in this country are frequently photographed before an important occasion so that their pictures can appear in the press. The Prince saw the photograph. It was late this afternoon. He noticed that I had—quite unwittingly—selected a costume similar to his own. I was driven to his house, and was begged not to go. I conceded to the request."

This was the moment when Warwick Hilling would normally have concluded the matter with a contemptuous shrug. Unfortunately, he was not in a position to shrug.

The two men consulted in low voices. Then Hilling was again questioned.

"But why do you not go in some other clothes, when you find out how it is?" came the inquiry.

"It was too late," replied Hilling.

"So! Then why do you stay at the house so long?"

"I was told that it would be dangerous to leave." Hilling was pleased with the way his mind was functioning. He was about to deliver a good point. "I was told that anyone seen in the Prince's clothes might be mistaken for the Prince, and shot at. And that, sir, appears to be true."

"Well, well, continue!" snapped the enemy.

"Continue? Have I not told you everything?" retorted Hilling. "I think it is now my turn to——"

"You have not told me where this ball is."

"Eh?"

"The ball you say you were going to?"

"Is that of importance, then?"

Hilling felt he was floundering again.

"If you cannot tell me, I may think it is!" What did the fellow mean by that? "To tell me will prove your story, so?"

Hilling fell into the trap. His brain was beginning to spin once more, and his cords bit into him.

"The Albert Hall!" he exclaimed, and swore at himself the next instant. But he had feared to hesitate any longer. That would have proved the importance of the information. And, when your interrogator has a revolver, he always wins in the end. . . .

The two men exchanged glances.

"And the Prince? Where is he? You have not told me that."

"You did not ask me that!"

"So! But now I ask it."

"Why should he tell me where he went?" But the revolver jabbed him again. "Very well, very well!" cried Hilling, desperately, making his last effort. "I will tell you! You force me! He has gone back to his country!" He paused, to try to mark the effect, but the faces of his hearers were mere movements in the smoky darkness. Had he seen them, he would have been disturbed by their smiles. In his ignorance he ran on, "Yes, that is what he has done, though I swore I would tell nobody. He went to the station—you will know which one, I do not—and I was to wait a while with his friend. Then his friend

would take me home, and would follow the Prince.
. . . Yes, but now he cannot!" cried Hilling, his
emotion suddenly rising. "For he is dead! And, by
God, sir——"

"Tch! Tch!" interrupted the enemy. "You talk
much, all of the sudden!" And then he laughed, and
suddenly Hilling found his face hovering palely over
him again. "A nice little story, so? And we go to the
station, so? Oh, no! Oh, no!" Hilling felt his
sleeve pinched viciously. "This clothes, where do you
find it, eh? You buy it, so?—what is the word—you
hire it, so?" He laughed again, and Hilling's blood
froze at the sound. "No, pig! This clothes is not
like the clothes of the Prince—it *is* the clothes of the
Prince! Do I not know?"

He leaped back. The other man had risen. Out of
the blackness came the final words:

"Ahi! It is plain! The Prince lend you his clothes.
The world—and me and my friend—we must think
you go to the ball, but you go to his house, and he go
to the ball. But why go to the ball, that is not so
plain, so you please tell us. Now spik quick, with
the one, two, three, becoss the time it go too fast.
Why did he go? One!"

"I don't know!" gasped Hilling.

"You do not know. So. The pistol, you can see it?
Why did he go? Two!"

"Damn you, I don't know!" shouted Hilling. "And if I did I wouldn't tell you!"

"Three and las', why did he go?"

Then Warwick Hilling laughed. He had come to the end of himself. The journey was completed. Every nerve in him had snapped, and he was roaring himself into Eternity. Ha, ha, ha, ha! This was funny! Ha, ha, ha, ha! He *didn't* know! Ha, ha, ha, ha! To sleep, to dream—now we'd learn! Ha, ha, ha, ha, ha——

A shot rang out. The laughter ceased. . . .

Three A.M.

"*Well!*" exclaimed the nymph. "And *where* have you been hiding yourself?"

Henry looked at her flushed, indignant face through a mist. Half a dozen hours ago he had never seen this girl; had not known of her existence; but now she came into his vision as from a long-forgotten past. No, not forgotten. She had been there, in his mind, all the while, but as a phantom, and between him and the phantom lay the reality of a dead man.

"What's the matter with you?" went on the nymph, as Henry merely stared at her. "Are you ill?"

"As a matter of fact," answered Henry simply, "I think I am."

"You certainly look it," she said. "Like me to see you home?"

But Henry jumped up.

"You would say that!" he cried. "You'd do anything for anybody, wouldn't you? Well—not this time. You'd better go away!"

She pushed him down again, then glanced anxiously

around. Fortunately nobody was near the spot, and the hysterical little outburst had not been overheard. Though, if it had been, it would not have occasioned more than the turn of a head and a smile. The nymph did not smile, however. She stared at her companion very hard, her prettily made-up eyes perplexed. The make-up was not so perfect as it had been. It had yielded a little to the ravages of carnival.

"Keep steady, Gauguin," she murmured, and put a hand to his forehead. "Hot! What's done it?"

"Didn't I tell you to go away?" replied Henry.

"Sickening for something? And think I'll catch it?"

"There you are!"

"In that case you certainly ought to go home, and *somebody's* got to take you."

"No, no, it's not that!" he exclaimed, as she seized his arm.

She laughed purposely. She wanted to ease the situation.

"I knew it wasn't," she answered, "though I will say you look like the morning after the night before. But what made you pretend?"

"Nothing."

"I see. And what made you leave me like that an hour ago?"

"Nothing, I tell you——"

"Nothing, nothing!" she retorted. "You're the rottenest liar I've ever struck. You need practice! Now, look here, Gauguin, I'm going to be severe with you, but it's for your own good. What the hell's the trouble? Sit up like a good boy and tell mummy!"

"But, I tell you—it *is* nothing—nothing to do with you, that is," exploded Henry, struggling against the knowledge that she was winning, and unable to determine whether he was glad or not. "Yes—since you will keep on—something has happened, but, don't you see, I want you to keep out of it!"

"Keep out of it," she repeated thoughtfully. "That's got a nasty sound. Have you been murdering anybody?"

"No!" he gasped.

"Well, that's a relief, anyway, because if you had it would have meant taking you back and hiding you under my bed! Awful prospect for a nice respectable girl like me. . . . But I'd have *done* it, Gauguin, because the only way to get a person like you to commit a murder would be to lay the body at your feet and give you a pistol and then pull the trigger for you. So now you know."

"You do make it difficult!" he muttered.

"If you weren't as blind as a bat, you'd see I'm trying to make it easy," she retorted. "You're the one that's making it difficult! P'r'aps you are as blind as

a bat? You haven't had anything more to drink,
have you?"

"Eh? As a matter of fact——"

"As a matter of fact, you have! I've got a new
name for you, Gauguin! Mr. As-a-matter-of-fact!"
She laughed and poked him. "Oh, my God, do smile!
Give us a bit of help! Somebody been getting after
you, is that it? Well, it's three o'clock, and this is
the time to look out for them! Oh, I say, Gauguin—
have you been a naughty boy?"

"No!" he shot back immediately.

"My, you are quick in the up-take!" she gasped.
"Well, we're clearing the board. You haven't murdered anyone, and you're still a virgin. Hooray, I've
made you look shocked! I wanted to, darling. You've
looked like a peahen with an earache much too long.
Now, then, have I got to go on guessing, or——"

"Wait a minute—I've got to think," interrupted
Henry.

"Two thinks are better than one," retorted the
nymph, "and you've had an hour all alone and got
nowhere. Where have you been?"

Where had he been? He hardly knew. At first, he
had suddenly lost his head, and fled from the Chinaman. He knew he had been an idiot the moment
afterward, but then he *was* an idiot. He had seen
the Chinaman turn as he had slipped away, and he

believed, though he had no proof, that the Chinaman
followed him. The belief, right or wrong, made him
lose his head again, and he had continued his flight,
behaving like a culprit as many an innocent man
had done before him. His sudden movement had upset
his control, and his mind became so jumbled that he
almost forgot what he was running away from. Was
it a Chinaman? Or a corpse? . . .

Then suddenly and startlingly he had seen the
corpse. He had stopped dead. The corpse was now
erect, and it had eyed him with an unwelcoming grin.

"Still running?" inquired the corpse.

It was the other coster.

The shock had temporarily bowled him over. The
coster had taken charge of him for a few minutes,
but had been only too glad to pass him on to a man
in a leopard skin who said he knew him.

"Then would you like him?" asked the other coster.

"Ol' friend of mine," babbled the man in the
leopard skin. "Gauguin."

It was the man in the leopard skin to whom Henry
had opened his eyes, and for a while he thought he
was back at the beginning again.

"What you want," said the leopard man, very earnestly, "is a drink."

The leopard man had had several.

Henry would have followed anybody's lead just

then. He only remembered the drink vaguely. Had there been more than one? He did not know. But some divine instinct—or perhaps it was just Henry Brown—saved him from reaching a condition that would have incapacitated him utterly till the morning, and suddenly he found himself running away again. He was running away, this time, from the man in the leopard skin and the condition of total incapacity for which he stood.

And then the nymph had slipped into his world again and had gradually made it solid once more . . . and here she was asking him to explain all these things!

"Thanks for all the information!" she smiled, breaking in on his silence with friendly sarcasm. "Perhaps it will come better after a cup of coffee."

There was a counter near them. She led him firmly to a seat at a small table, and brought the coffee herself.

"I'm all right now," he said. "I didn't know people like you lived."

"Florence Nightingale isn't in it," she replied. "Idiot!"

She made him drink his coffee. Her practical behavior and her refusal to be morbid slapped him back into activity. The coffee also helped.

"You really want to hear?" he warned her.

"I'm *going* to hear," she answered, "if I have to use

a corkscrew. You went after that coster chap, didn't you?"

"Yes."

"And I went after *you,* but was just too late to catch you. Did you find him?"

"Yes."

"Where?"

"In—in some dark place or other."

"Sounds sweet!"

"Please don't joke."

"All right, I won't, but what happened? Did you—go for each other?"

"No."

"Well, that's one good thing. The first thing I looked for was bruises. What did you say to him?"

"I—I didn't say anything to him."

"Why not?"

"He was lying on the ground."

"Oh! He'd been drinking, too?" He did not reply. Suddenly she read his expression. She gave a little gasp, but quickly recovered herself. "You know, Gauguin, it *is* time you got home!" she said, very soberly.

Equally soberly he now answered her.

"He was dead," he said.

"How did you know he was?" she retorted.

"I could tell."

"In the condition I found you in, Gauguin, I don't think you could tell anything!"

"But I wasn't in that condition then," replied Henry, smiling faintly. "It—it was that—the shock, I expect—that made me go off the reel. You see, afterward——"

"Yes?" she prompted, for he had paused.

"Well, I met a Chinaman chap—I think he saw me coming away—but I don't know—and he stopped me for a light. And then he said a funny thing. He said, 'Have you taken any good photographs?' Oh," he added, as he noticed her blank expression, "I forgot to tell you. Just before I found the—the coster chap, I found this."

He pulled the camera out of his pocket.

"Where?" she frowned.

"On the ground. Near the—the body."

"But why——"

"Why did I bring it away with me? Because I'm a mug! As a matter of fact, I didn't know I had the beastly thing till that Chinaman asked his question—and there it was, sticking half out as large as life. I expect I put it in without thinking when I got the shock."

"Well. Then what did you do?"

Henry colored.

"It's easy to see why people lie," he said, "but I'm

not going to—to you. I couldn't, somehow. But now that good opinion you had of me will go west, only don't forget I knew you were wrong from the start."

"Do you mean, you did a bunk?" asked the nymph.

"Good guess," he replied.

"Easy guess! I'd have done a bunk myself! And then I suppose you went quite woolly, and hid in cloakrooms and lavatories and things!"

"Something like that. But what really knocked me over was a ghastly shock I got when I thought I saw the dead chap walking up to me. Of course, it was only another fellow dressed like a coster. I—I—really, I think I fainted. How's that for a girlish thing to do? And somebody gave me too many drinks——"

"Damn fools!"

"No, I was the damn fool. Anyhow, that part of it's over, and now I suppose I'll have to report the matter to somebody or other."

"You'll do nothing of the sort!" she returned, sharply. "You wanted to keep *me* out of it—well, I'm going to keep *you* out of it! It's nothing to do with you! We're going to leave this place right now."

"No, we can't do that—I mean, I can't do that!" interrupted Henry earnestly. "You see—I think I know who did it!"

"What!" gasped the nymph.

He nodded, and gave a little gulp himself.

"Yes—that's a bit nasty, but there it is. One can't keep a thing like that back, can one? You see, I'd seen this chap alive a few minutes before—he'd stuck his head out of a passage—and then I saw two people go through the passage after him. A man and a woman, in sort of historical costumes. And when they came out—one at a time—they looked green. I could identify them both. The woman didn't see me, she was too upset, but the man, he came out last and, well, he looked ghastly, too, but when he saw me he pretended to be cool and lit a cigarette. Now, then, I've told you the lot. *Can* I let it go at that?"

"Yes, you're jolly well going to let it go at that!" answered the nymph. "I've only known you a few hours, Gauguin, but I've known you long enough to like you—no, don't interrupt, let me speak for a bit— to like you, and to understand you! You're the kind of innocent person who blunders into trouble, and if you don't drop this right now, you can take it from me you'll end in *real* trouble this time, all right! You know why I first joined up with you here, don't you? To look after you. Well, I'm going to play my stroke through. We're going down right now to get your coat!"

Henry removed his eyes from her and fixed them on the ground. Her words swam warmly round him, giving him sensations that were new to him. He was receiving something he had never received before, a woman's protective interest. A light smile was all he had dared to expect from the Albert Hall, a trivial glance that he could have carried home with him and exalted in his imagination. But this was something bigger. He did not over-estimate it. He dwelt on it soberly, and saw it for just what it was; but that was enough to give him a perilous inclination to cry. He wanted to go home—to be taken home. There was no more harmony for him here, among all these pleasure-seeking crowds. A quiet ending, that would wipe out the nightmare of the last hour. . . . He was very tired.

But could the easy path be traveled? Was it really as easy as all that? Quite apart from the uncomfortable sense that it had not been earned, that it savored too much of running away, would it put "Finis" to the nightmare? After his idiotic behavior, might it not be a direct incitement to the nightmare to follow him?

"You've forgotten this," said Henry, taking the camera from his pocket.

"Quick, put it back!" the nymph whispered to him sharply.

In the distance she had suddenly spotted a Chinaman.

"Lost your handkerchief, Sis?" inquired Conrad. "Allow me to lend you mine!"

"What makes you think I need a handkerchief?" retorted Dorothy.

"A time comes in the lives of all dancers when humidity invades the brow," he answered. "One arrives dignified and dry, and leaves weary and wet."

"Speak for yourself," suggested Dorothy.

"True," nodded Conrad. "And, after all, man mops, while woman plies the puff. But you haven't asked the most important question."

"What?"

"How do I know you - have lost your handkerchief?"

"Well, if it amuses you—how do you?"

"Because," grinned Conrad, "I saw the Prince of Ruritania pick it up. Just after your dance with him. I'm not sure he didn't make you drop it, so he could pay a call here and return it! I'll bet he does, too!"

"How do you know he hasn't already?" asked his sister. "You've only just returned to the box yourself."

"Yes, where have you been all this while?" added Mrs. Shannon, and turned to her husband and Lankester. "The way that boy flies away after he has finished with me! He's very good, and asks me to dance most politely, but the moment the music stops he leaps off as though that's that!"

"Oh, Mother!" expostulated Conrad. "Do I? I don't mean it! Let's go out and have a dance now, shall we?"

"No, thank you. I believe we're *all* puffed, if we admitted it. Anyway, I know I am. But where *have* you been?"

"Ah!" murmured Conrad mysteriously.

"Found one at last?" inquired Dorothy.

"Don't be vulgar," said Conrad. "I've been engaged on secret-service work!"

"I must watch your career," laughed Lankester. "You may grow up useful, after all. What sort of secret-service work? Diplomatic?"

"I think I'd better warn you," answered Conrad, with engaging frankness, "I'm no good at it. Give me a chap to knock down, and if he's smaller than I am I'll do it with ease. But when it comes to looking for anybody, I'm a failure."

"You mean, if the anybody is male," commented Dorothy.

"Well, I like that!" exclaimed Conrad. "Wouldn't you think I was the World's Roué, the way she talks! But I suppose sisters are sisters all the world over. The person I was looking for, Madame du Barry, *was* a male—so of course *you* ought to have been sent on the hunt!"

"May we know the identity?" asked Lankester, amused.

"Why not?" replied Conrad. "A coster."

Mr. Shannon sat very still. He stared out of the box across the hall, his eyes unseeing.

"What on earth set you off chasing costers?" demanded Lankester.

"I hope it wasn't the one who was in that fight," added Mrs. Shannon.

"It was," admitted Conrad, "and it was Sweet Nell of Old Drury who set me off chasing him. But you needn't worry, Mother—I didn't find him. He seems to have vanished into the void. And so does Sweet Nell herself—I can't find her anywhere, and I want to report failure."

"You stay in the box and cool down!" snapped Mr. Shannon, suddenly and unexpectedly. He felt that if this conversation went on much longer he would burst. "You'll be getting into trouble!"

His tone grated. "James is getting tired," thought Mrs. Shannon. "I wonder if I oughtn't to get him home. . . . Yes, but the children won't want to leave. . . ." Meanwhile Conrad remonstrated.

"Oh, I say, do I ever get into trouble?" he exclaimed. "Why is everybody dropping on me? I'm most model! Yes, and I'm ready to bet that Nell

Gwynn is, too, beneath the paint and the powder. You may not think it, but I'm a *judge!*"

"Yes, I'm sure you are, dear," interposed Mrs. Shannon soothingly, "and I'm sure that this Nell Gwynn you're talking about is perfectly prim and proper. But I still don't see why you should neglect your own party to go and find a coster for her?"

"She's lost him," explained Conrad. "But when I offered myself as a substitute she gently but firmly refused. . . . There you are, Dad, if she'd been the kind that gets you into trouble she'd have jumped at the chance of dancing with a young and innocent like me! . . . But, no! She refuses. And all I could do was to extract a half-promise that she would give me a dance if I found her coster. Yes," he went on, with a sudden grin, "and all *I* could do was to half-find the coster."

"What's that?" cried Mr. Shannon.

"Yes, and that nearly *did* land me into trouble," said Conrad, while Mrs. Shannon gave another anxious look at her husband. "I had a bit of a shock. You see there he was—perfectly still—but somehow *different*. I'd seen him before, you know, and he'd been a quick, nervous sort of chap—always moving or twitching or something—but now he seemed kind of stiff. However, I went up to him and gave him a slap on the back. He moved then all right! He swung round and made a breeze that blew me half a mile. 'What the naughty word are you doing?' he shouted. And then I found out that he was *another* coster, and that he'd been taken for the other coster before, and that he had lumbago, and that if it ever happened again he'd jolly well kill somebody!" He laughed. "Well, there's one thing. If that first coster's found dead, we'll know who's done it!"

He turned and grinned at his father. He hated rows, though he didn't believe in giving way to one's fear of them, and he wanted to dissipate the rather mysterious sultriness that had come upon his paternal parent. It was mysterious because, dash it all, didn't one go to the Chelsea Arts Ball for a bit of mild fun, and had not this very Nell Gwynn smiled at his father and received a smile back? Well, then. . . . But Mr. Shannon was not attending. He was staring out of the box again into the body of the hall.

Conrad's grin dissolved. Well, well, he'd find his niche someday, he supposed, but meanwhile life was rather a swot when the only times people thought you were *really* funny were when you tried to be serious.

But after all, reflected Conrad, as his idle gaze followed his father's, wasn't life a swot to everybody? Dad had come here to enjoy himself, and look at him! Ditto mother—and look at her! Somehow, he didn't think she was having a really good time. Sis—up and

down. Probably enjoying it, but as nervous as an old
lady with a trunk. Harold—he stole a quick look at
Harold, for whom he had a secret admiration—grave
as an owl. Wasn't there a middle point somewhere
between all this sort of thing and—he gazed into the
ballroom again—*that* sort of thing?

And then, all at once, his semi-philosophic mood
vanished. At last his eyes had spotted the lady of his
momentary thoughts. He jumped to his feet.

"My God, what's the matter with the boy!" jerked
Mr. Shannon.

"Do sit down, dear," begged Mrs. Shannon.

"No, I have seen the lovely Nell!" cried Conrad.
"Watch me report my failure to her, and see how
well we both behave! Yes, and look who's with her!"
he added. "Dorothy, it's your Prince of Ruritania.
Any message for him?"

The next moment he was out of the box.

"Time is passing," said a voice in Sally's ear.

She turned her head. The Prince was regarding her
gravely. Ever since she had entered the hall—only
a few hours ago, but they seemed like days—she had
been supremely conscious of his dominating personality. There had been other personalities with which,
till now, she had been more actively concerned—her
working partner, Sam, and her victim, Mr. Shannon—

but they had been dwarfed in her mind beside the Prince, and were, indeed, mere stepping-stones. For Sally was not thinking in terms of L.S.D. Within her lurked the ambition of the real Nell Gwynn, and of Madame du Barry, and of La Pompadour, and of all the other famous mistresses who were represented here because, through some special quality, they had risen out of the obscurity of dark streets into the strange fame of history, and had clouded their sins in great audacity.

This was the first time Sally had spoken with the Prince tonight. She had had one previous conversation in a dance hall, where a little foreigner had addressed her at her table and had presented her bluntly with five pounds "just for a little talk, good, so?" The little talk had been mysterious and exciting. It had ended at another table, where she had met the Prince.

Here the proposition was made, and definite details were discussed. The Prince at first had mainly listened, with a rather sad acceptance of a sordid proposition (if Sally could read his attitude aright), while the little foreigner talked, and while Sally herself agreed. At the very end, the Prince had suddenly looked at her, as though noticing her personally for the first time, and had said, "It is settled? You consent, then?" "I'll do my part, if King Charles will do his," she had answered. "He will do his. That we know by his little private diary," interposed the little foreigner. "Our spy, he search for one thing, and he find another that give me the, how you say, brainwave!" He tapped his forehead importantly. "And you, voilà, my second brainwave!" "The second brainwave is even better than the first," the Prince had then concluded, rising. "King Charles will be a man of iron, mademoiselle, if you fail—and, therefore, quite unlike King Charles. Till the Albert Hall, then, though remember we meet there as strangers until you hand me what you are asked to procure."

Then he had held out his hand, and as she had taken it she had asked, "And that will be the end?" He had not replied. He had merely smiled. And Sally had built on that smile. The Prince also, she decided, would have to be a man of iron. . . .

And now here he was, addressing her again—and she was unable to hand him what she had been asked to procure!

"Where can we talk?" she murmured, in reply to his remark.

"Why not here, surrounded by people whose ears are closed to all but their own poor nonsense?" he suggested.

As she hesitated, he went on, his quiet smooth voice acting on her almost soporifically:

"You know who I am? I am Mr. Warwick Hilling, an actor, who now breaks a vow of silence because his head has been turned by the beautiful Nell Gwynn. What more natural?"

"Mr. Hilling might prefer a secluded couch?" she suggested, half-provocatively, half-practically.

"That is good reasoning," admitted the Prince, "although, were I not Mr. Hilling, but somebody emulating him, I might think that spies are less liable to search in the open than in the places where there are secluded couches. Still, Fate, not ourselves, will decide our issue for us. It will be this or that. So let us move to your secluded couch, in the belief that the choice is our own."

"You speak English well," she commented, as they began to walk away.

"I have studied in England," he answered. "English and French, they are the necessary languages."

They were not destined to reach the secluded couch without interruption. Just as they were leaving the ballroom a youth in somewhat bedraggled gold came bounding up to them. He sent a grin of recognition to the Prince, then banished the grin and addressed Sally with a woebegone expression.

"No luck!" he exclaimed. "I couldn't find your coster friend anywhere!"

"Well, never mind," answered Sally quickly.

"I can't help minding," replied the youth. "It's lost me my chance of a dance!"

"Perhaps—another time," said Sally, longing to get rid of him, but again disturbed by his ingenuousness. "It was very good of you to look. Thank you very much."

"Not at all—a pleasure," murmured the youth. "I'll still keep my eyes open. Oh, by the way, I'd better warn you—there's another coster knocking around, but he's not the same one. He's got lumbago and a temper, and the combination produceth fireworks."

If he had received any encouragement he might have lingered, but Sally's smile was merely polite, and the Prince made no attempt to smile at all.

"Oh, well, I'll toddle off now," concluded Conrad sadly, "but I thought I'd just come along and report, you know." He turned and vanished.

The Prince made no comment until they had found their quiet spot. Then he asked:

"This coster? Is it the man who has been working with you?"

"Yes," replied Sally.

"And it is true—you cannot find him?"

"If I could have found him, you'd have heard from me before now! He's disappeared!"

"Without completing his work?" inquired the Prince, gravely. "That is a pity."

"He did complete his work," returned Sally, frowning. "All but one thing. He—he took the photograph——" The Prince's eyes grew suddenly bright. "Yes, but now I can't find him."

"Do we need him?"

"No, but we need the camera. The film is inside."

"Ah," murmured the Prince. "Then he must be found."

Sally looked at him desperately. Her mind was in conflict. She was torn between a sense of failure, and a desire for failure. She wished she could have met the Prince in entirely different circumstances, and that this hateful business had not been the cause of it. For a moment, as his eyes rested on hers, she wondered. . . .

"Undoubtedly, he must be found," repeated the Prince.

"I have searched for over an hour," answered Sally.

"And so, I understand, has your young friend," said the Prince, with a faint smile at last. "Was that wise?"

"No, thoroughly unwise," retorted Sally defiantly. "If you want me to tell you the truth, Prince, your ambassador, or secretary, or whatever he calls himself, picked out the wrong person for the job! I loathe and detest it—now that I've done it—and if that displeases you, I can't help it!"

"It does not displease me," replied the Prince evenly, after a little pause. "On the contrary, it gratifies me. We can now converse with greater understanding. I, too, dislike this affair. There is a smell of stinking fish in it. When my agent proposed it, I hesitated. But everything else had failed, and——" He shrugged his shoulders. "It is to save bloodshed. A hundred, a thousand, ten thousand lives may be saved by this thing you loathe and detest so rightly. A kingdom, also—if that matters. . . . So my agent argued, when I hesitated. And so I argue, now that you hesitate. Do I convert you back again? I hope so."

"What happens, if you do?" she asked.

"We continue our search," answered the Prince.

"And after that?"

"After that? You look ahead! If we are successful, the rest is with me."

"You and Mr. Shannon?"

"Yes."

"He's a poor old fool, Prince, you can take it from me!"

"A poor old fool can be, also, a dangerous old fool. He can, through his folly and his selfishness, imperil countless lives. I do not speak as one who is himself beyond folly. But sometimes the big problem comes— we find ourselves face to face with it—and we try to escape from the folly that is too great and that spells ruin. Yes, we try. Perhaps we succeed, perhaps we do not. If we do not, we return to our folly, and dip our swords in blood. You do not understand these things. Forgive me. I have said more than I meant. . . . So much more," he added, almost whimsically, "that I do not agree my agent picked wrongly when he picked you for this business. You draw one out, and make one say, without regret, the word too much!"

Sally frowned at the compliment, and bit her lip.

"Should I feel flattered?" she demanded.

"Do you not?" he asked.

"I don't know," she answered bluntly. "But I wish we hadn't met just like this. Well, let's get on with it. But it's up to you now, Prince, for I haven't an idea in my head."

"Perhaps I can get the idea, if you will tell me what has happened?" he suggested. "Remember, I know nothing. No details, I mean."

"That's true," she nodded. "Well, here is the story."

She gave him a rapid account of the circumstances. He listened without interruption. When she had finished he said:

"The idea is obvious."

"Is it? Then I'd like you to explain it!"

"We must return to the spot where you say the picture was taken——"

"I've been back there."

"And searched thoroughly?"

"No—o," she admitted, after a moment's thought. "I just poked my head in."

"He could be hiding, then, and you would not see him."

"Why should he hide?"

"Why, if he does not hide, does he not appear? But I agree there may be another reason, and it is because of this other reason that I say we shall return to the spot."

"What's the other reason?"

"An—accident."

Sally started. It was odd, but she had never thought of that! She pondered for a moment on the possibility. But—what sort of an accident?

"You were the first to leave, you tell me?"

"Yes. I got out as soon as I could!"

"Then Mr. Shannon was still there, with the photographer?"

"I suppose so. Yes, of course."

"And Mr. Shannon would probably be angry?" She stared at him. "Very angry indeed, one cannot doubt."

Sally gasped, as the horrible idea entered into her. She did not believe it. She did not believe that Mr. Shannon, even in a fit of frenzy, was either courageous or fool enough to commit murder, nor did she believe that Sam was incapable of looking after himself. But the mere possibility froze her blood, and rendered her momentarily incapable of speech.

"So I think there is little doubt about our next step," the Prince continued quietly. "You will show me where this place is, and I will find out whether the photographer is still there."

Then suddenly Sally found her voice.

"It may be a risk," she said.

"If it is, there is no need for two to take it," he answered. "Can you tell me the way, so that I can find it for myself?"

But Sally shook her head at that. She was sure she could not tell him the way so that he could find it for himself, and she was sure she would not have done so if she could. There was no altruism in her attitude. Horrible curiosity and the fear of waiting were at the bottom of it. Perhaps she also had the subconscious thought that a risk shared forms the best cement of friendship.

Now they left the ground floor of the hall, and mounted to the higher regions. It was strange to realize that, with the majority of people they went by, the business of merry-making was pursuing its unin-

terrupted course, and that other minds had no realization of drama and tragedy. Yet to Sally, as she led
her companion up stone staircases and along curved
corridors, it was the merry-making that was the un-
real thing. Joy did not reside inside these walls for
her—it was a prize she hoped for when she had
escaped from them. . . .

"Here," said Sally.

The Prince looked toward the dark slit of a passage.

"You will wait?" he asked.

"No, thank you! I'm coming, too."

The Prince nodded, accepting her attitude. Then
he gave a quick glance round. Nobody was in sight.

The next moment he was in the passage. He had
moved silently but with disconcerting swiftness, and
she darted after him in a panic. In the passage he
paused, and she nearly ran into his back. Now they
moved slowly into the dim, unpalatable space. She
shuddered as she encountered its familiar twists and
turns and sudden steps. In a few short hours they had
become painfully recognizable.

"Be careful!" she whispered.

"Where were you—then?" he whispered back.

She stretched forward a hand, took his arm, and
directed it toward the spot. A faint gray line might
have indicated the step on which she had sat with Mr.
Shannon.

"And the photographer, where was he?" came the Prince's soft voice again through the darkness.

Once more she directed his arm.

"Ah—lower down," murmured the Prince, and began cautiously to descend.

This time she did not accompany him. She waited, while his vague form dropped lower and lower into the pit. Then she heard a scratch, followed by a little spurt of flame. Now the top half of him became a black smudge against a flickering outline of yellow light. The smudge bent down. The movement produced a large, outrageous shadow that appeared to have been born a mile off, and that nearly made Sally shriek.

"Hold on, it'll soon be over!" she thought, to steady herself.

The black smudge remained in its bent position for a nerve-racking time. Was it ever going to move again? It was perfectly motionless. But the shadow moved, as the matchlight flickered. . . .

The light went out.

"For God's sake!" gasped Sally, the situation beating her.

She did not know that the figure below her turned swiftly at her exclamation, for in the sudden darkness it was blotted out completely; but she heard the sound that came a second or two later. A dull, distant thud, as of a body landing somewhere. She gave a little scream. It was stopped by a hand over her mouth.

"Come away quickly," whispered a voice in her ear.

It was—thank God!—the Prince's voice. How had he leaped up to her side so quickly? She had believed at first that the thud was the sound of his own body, and that he had fallen. It was that that had made her scream. But somebody else's body must have fallen, and the Prince must have started his own movement toward her before the sound had broken into the stillness.

They were out in the light again. Nobody was near. The Prince was walking coolly by her side.

"A cigarette is good for the nerves, I think," he said.

She took one from his case. It was the same case that had been held out, some hours earlier, to a needy actor who at that moment was passing through an even worse experience. As the Prince struck a match, she remembered too vividly the last time he had struck one, and her cigarette trembled between her lips.

They walked on for a while without speaking. The Prince was also smoking. Then he suddenly stopped. They were standing in the bend of one of the smaller staircases.

"I think we part here," he said.

"Part?" she repeated, in astonishment.

"I think it is best," he answered.

"But—why?" she demanded.

"There is nothing more for you to do," he replied. "The rest is now for me. Do not look any more for the photographer. Do not look for the camera. Go home. And presently you will hear from me." She glanced at him sharply, but his next words disappointed her. "You will receive your recompense."

"You mean my pay?" she exclaimed, with a sort of bitter bluntness.

"As agreed," he nodded.

"I see—and that will be the end of it?"

"Let us hope so." Was he willfully misunderstanding her? "Indeed, we must make sure that it is."

She shrugged her shoulders as she asked—almost mechanically, for she knew the answer—"Well, who was it? You had better tell me."

"The man we went to look for."

"I guessed it. And he was—dead?"

The Prince nodded.

"I hope——" he began gravely, but she interrupted him, again knowing what he was going to say.

"He was nothing to me. We used to work together once, but that was all over—and this was just for old lang syne. A mistake, too." She paused, then added, grimly, "Queer business! But for this, I don't know what I'd have done with him tonight. He was being a trouble."

"You mean he wanted too big a share?"

"Damn sight too big! He wanted *me!*"

She tried not to redden under the Prince's thoughtful stare. Some people passed by. When they had gone, and the footsteps and voices had ceased to echo, the Prince said quietly:

"I will forget that."

"What do you mean?" asked Sally.

"And you had better forget it, too. You did not kill him——"

"God, no!"

"But, if he had persisted?" Sally's heart missed a beat. "I see now you understand what I mean. Yes, and why I wish you to go home now, and leave the rest to me."

"I'm not so sure about that," replied Sally, frowning. "You didn't kill him either."

"Undoubtedly I did not. He was dead when I came upon him. He was hanging over the bottom stair. When you exclaimed I turned too quickly in the dark, and shifted the body. It fell down into some pit or well or space, who knows what?"

"Then who *did* kill him?" inquired Sally, after a short pause. "Or—don't we inquire?"

"I think that depends," replied the Prince. "Suicide? Perhaps. An accident? More likely, an accident. The coroner can decide. Unless, of course, the police are informed that Mr. Shannon was last seen with the deceased, and it is suggested that they look for a camera. I myself found no camera."

"Of course—Mr. Shannon's got it!" muttered Sally.

"Or it has got Mr. Shannon's fingerprints," answered the Prince. "In any case, I do not think he would welcome a police search. So, after all—though at a cost—the night may prove productive."

Suddenly Sally thought of the cost, lying silently in the darkness.

"We haven't much pity!" she said.

"When we desire a thing above all else we have none," he answered. "Did I have pity for you?"

That time Mr. Warwick Hilling should have died. The bullet missed his body by an inch. But he paid it the compliment of passing through all the agony of death, merely escaping the death itself, for the bullet pinged so close that he felt its passage, and the violent snapping of something preceded a complete collapse of his physical structure.

It was with the utmost amazement, therefore, that he found he could still contemplate himself after the violence of the explosion, and that this contemplation was taking place not from some celestial cloud, but from earth.

"I am alive!" he thought, coming out of his swoon. "No, I am not! Yes, I am! Oh, nonsense!"

This line of argument did not advance him far. He flew to Shakespeare. " 'There are more things in Heaven and Earth, Horatio, than are dreamt of in our philosophy!' " This, undoubtedly, was one of them.

"I am not dead," he decided at last. He decided aloud, for the sound of his rather rich voice comforted him. "I was shot at, but the bullet missed. 'Thus by a chance too fragile to be reckoned, Are we to Harmony or Discord beckoned.' Yes, but if the bullet missed me, why did I snap? Why do I feel as though I had become—unknit?"

He repeated the word "unknit." Then he substituted the word "undone." The substitution was the subconscious device of a clearing mind to interpret the truth. Warwick Hilling sat up.

"I *am* undone!" he said.

The top portion of him was, at any rate. The bullet had snapped not a rib, but a cord.

Complete release, nevertheless, was not achieved without a long and tiring struggle. At various other portions of his anatomy Hilling was firmly tied, and his strength was at a low ebb. His fingers were numb.

So were his legs. But on his side were patience and a certain knowledge of knots, acquired in the performance of the Houdini trick, plus the excellent start given to him by the surprisingly friendly bullet; and the struggle ended at last, and he stumbled out of his cords.

He continued to stumble till he reached a wall. He felt his way along it to a door. As was to be expected, the door was locked.

To force the door seemed far beyond his strength, but he might have tried it had not a vague brightening in the darkness attracted his eye to a point on the wall farthest from the door, a little distance above his height. If this was a window, it was a peculiarly dim one. If it was not a window, what was it?

He groped his way back across the room. He found that it was a window. Pushing a table under it—the table to which he had been bound—he stood up and easily reached the ledge. Then the reasons for the dimness were revealed to him. There was a brick wall immediately opposite the window, only a few feet away. This and the fog almost blotted the window out.

He smashed the window by poking a chair-leg through it. He ducked the splinters, though they all fell outward. Then he opened the window's frame, and found that he need not have broken the glass at all. The window opened quite easily, inward, and there was just room, he estimated, for his form to pass through.

Now came an operation that appealed to his dramatic sense, if not to his sense of personal comfort. He was not going to risk a twenty-foot drop. Gathering up the cords that had bound him, he put them to a new use. One end he secured to the window-frame. The other was thrown out into the unknown. He had once performed a similar feat on the stage, but then he had descended onto a convenient mattress.

He followed the rope into the unknown, gripping it tight and allowing his feet to dangle before beginning the perilous descent. Then his dramatic sense received a shock. His feet dangled promptly onto stone flooring.

"So all I need have done," he reflected, "was to open the window and step out. Well, well."

The stone flooring was a step. The steps went up the side of the wall which contained the window, and apparently led from an area to the street. Warwick Hilling mounted to a railing, passed through, and found himself once more on solid pavement.

Now, at last, he was free to do as he liked, and merely had to decide what to do. For a moment even that seemed difficult. Then he decided on a policeman. He was not in the best costume to interview policemen, but that could not be helped.

For once luck favored him. He floundered into a burly form round the first corner. Or *was* it luck? The policeman's attitude was not promising.

"Hallo! What's this?" he demanded.

Hilling had never found a simple question more difficult to answer. For a few moments his mind went blank, while the policeman's attitude became less and less promising.

"Been merrymaking?" said the policeman grimly.

The unconscious irony of the question loosened Hilling's tongue.

"If being nearly murdered is merrymaking," he answered, "I have been merrymaking."

"What's that?" asked the policeman sharply.

"I am telling you that I have been nearly murdered," repeated Hilling.

The constable eyed his costume, much of the glory of which had departed, formed his own conclusions, and remarked:

"Been in a scrap, eh? Well, what about going home now and forgetting it?"

"Listen, constable! I have to get to the Albert Hall——"

"Oh, Albert Hall," interposed the policeman. "I see. Well, you're a bit off your beat, so I wouldn't try to get back there. 'Specially in this fog."

"Yes, yes, but I've *got* to get back!" cried Hilling. "And you've got to go back with me!"

"Now, then, *what's* all this about?" inquired the policeman, with watchful patience.

"The people who tried to kill me—in a house right near here—you must forgive me if I am a little incoherent, but my brain—yes, they are now on their way to the Albert Hall to kill someone else. They may have arrived——"

"Steady, steady," interrupted the policeman, who imagined he knew the reason for his queer companion's incoherency and the state of his brain. "They? Who are they? Let's hear, sir."

"I—I don't know."

"Ah, that's a pity."

"Excepting that they are foreigners."

"Oh?" The policeman frowned. "Well, and who's this person you say they're after?"

"I—again, constable, I do not know."

"It seems to me, sir, that you don't know very much——"

"Wait a moment, wait a moment!" interrupted Hilling testily. "How can I tell you my story when you continually interrupt? And with my head spinning like this? I have been shot at. I have been within an ace of death. And you expect—well, well! This other man—I can tell you this, at any rate. He is dressed in my costume——"

"Well, what's that you've got on? His?" interposed

the policeman, with an ominous lessening of patience. "I suppose you know who *you* are, anyway?"

Hilling drew himself up to his full height.

"I am Mr. Warwick Hilling," he answered, and since the information made no impression, he added, "An actor of, I think I may say, some note."

"Yes, well, we don't want any acting in the street——" began the constable.

This was too much. Indignation blazed, and for a moment gave a weak but outraged man the ascendancy.

"What the Hades——! Haven't you any brain at all?" cried Hilling, with desperate anger. "Can't you understand, Thick-skull, that I am trying to tell you something—that I am in no condition—— There has been an attempt to murder me, in a house in this block. There is now to be an attempt—I firmly believe—to murder somebody else for whom *I* was mistaken. There, sir, is *that* clear? At the Albert Hall. And another man has already been murdered——"

"Hey! Another?" exclaimed the constable, perking up.

"I have interested you at last," observed Hilling icily.

"We'll see about that," retorted the policeman. "Murder committed already, eh? In a house in this block? Well, take me along——"

"No, no, not in that house," said Hilling.

"Where, then."

"Eh? In another house."

"Well, where's this other house?"

"I don't know."

"Oh, you don't? H'm. Who's the person who's been murdered, then?"

"I—I don't know. That is——"

"A party you don't know has been murdered in a house you don't know, and now another party you don't know is going to be murdered in the Albert Hall! I think the best thing, sir, will be for you to step along to the station. P'r'aps that'll clear your mind a bit!"

The suggestion was really a sensible one, for Hilling was telling his story in a most unsatisfactory manner, but as the constable laid hold of his sleeve a sudden panic seized him, and Warwick Hilling did a very foolish thing. He interpreted the constable's action as a threat, and struck him.

The blow was too effective. The policeman, thoroughly unprepared, staggered back and sat down. By the time he had risen to his feet Warwick Hilling had vanished.

The policeman blew his whistle. In due course he managed to connect up with two or three other policemen, who were instructed to assist in a search for a pugnacious lunatic. A man who said he was a bloody actor, who looked like a bloody Turk, but who, in the heated opinion of the constable who had interviewed him, was bloody well neither!

The search continued indignantly through the fog, and the fog won.

Four A.M.

THE nymph and Henry were still sitting at their little table. The Chinaman had not seen them—that time—his attention having been diverted by a portly representation of Henry VIII who had suddenly and massively stepped on his toe. The incident had caused the Chinaman to retreat, presumably to seek first aid or to have a good cry, and the anxious couple who had watched the retreat with relief had resumed their discussion.

Then had followed a state of deadlock from which had emerged their present compromise. The nymph's desire to leave was countered by Henry's argument that, quite apart from any ethical consideration, this might be a most suspicious move to make. Ten to one Henry would be followed—he was convinced that the Chinaman was a detective—and then what would he be able to say for himself? But every time Henry urged, with decreasing enthusiasm, that it was his duty to report his gruesome discovery, the nymph countered with all the arguments she could think of. He would

252

probably get innocent people into trouble, she said, because, of course, he would have to mention the historical lady and gentleman, and most likely they had nothing whatever to do with it. He would probably get himself into trouble, because look how long he had already waited, and that was almost as suspicious as going home. He would probably get *her* into trouble, because he could say what he liked, she wasn't going to leave him! And then suppose somebody else had already reported the matter? Or if they hadn't yet, suppose they presently did? In that case there would probably be no need for them to have anything to do with it at all. Oh, yes, of course, there was the camera. But mightn't somebody else have dropped it? Or couldn't it have been picked up anywhere? Never trouble trouble till trouble troubles you—that was the nymph's motto.

Henry was both consoled and confused when she admitted quite honestly that she didn't care a rap about the ethical side of the question. It is usual to invest one's goddess with the highest moral qualities, and Henry was discovering more rapidly, perhaps, than most, that he must go on loving his goddess without them. It humiliated him to realize that he could do this with perfect ease.

And thus they had agreed at last to sit where they were, do nothing, and see what happened.

For a long while nothing happened. They chatted with a sort of forced gaiety, conscious of each other's effort, or fell into heavy silences. One silence lasted for nearly twenty minutes. Henry felt as though he were chained to his chair. Evidently the nymph felt the same way about it, for all at once she raised her moody, sleepy eyes and laughed.

"Well, what about it?" she said. "Are we booked for the duration?"

"Looks like it," answered Henry.

"That means another hour," she replied, glancing at her wrist watch. "We'll be turned out at five. My God, Gauguin, it's almost time to get up, and we haven't yet gone to bed!"

He looked at her with sudden sympathy. She was a nymph at 4:00 A.M., if a somewhat bedraggled nymph—but what would the nymph have to become at 9:00 A.M.? A girl behind a counter. . . .

"I say, you *must* go home!" he exclaimed.

"What's wrong with both?" she retorted.

He might have yielded that time. But a blue-clad figure loomed over them, and then slid into a seat.

"This is quite, quite unwarrantable," said the China-man. "But—I wonder—*might* I see that camera?"

"Eh?" jerked Henry, his wits dissipated by the suddenness of the question. "Camera?"

"Yes, that's what I said," answered the Chinaman, eying Henry's telltale pocket.

The nymph kept her head. She turned toward the Chinaman and fixed him with her gaze until he became conscious of it.

"I suppose you know, young man," she remarked severely, "that you are being exceedingly rude?"

"Am I?" replied the Chinaman. "I'm sorry. But do people have manners at fancy dress balls? I don't think I've noticed it." Something in his expression as he continued to regard the nymph annoyed Henry. "King Henry VIII stamped on my foot some while ago, and he just smiled and said, 'All in the night's work.'"

"He's drunk!" exclaimed the nymph, turning back to Henry. Neither of the two men guessed how her little heart was thumping. "Come along—if *he* won't move, *we* can!"

"I would know the camera," persisted the Chinaman. "No. 1a Pocket Kodak Junior, Anastigmat lens, F. 7.7., 131 mm. Fastest exposure, one fiftieth. Smallest stop, 45. Focus by turning the lens, range 5 feet to 100."

The nymph had seized Henry's arm, but Henry did not move. He knew that, whatever this was, it would have to be faced.

"Do you mean you have lost a camera?" he demanded.

"It sounds rather like it," answered the Chinaman. "But, of course, you may say there are thousands of cameras answering this description. Certainly. Not, however, with a special mark upon them. Now I could tell you in half a second whether your camera has that special mark. I put it on all my cameras."

"Oh—you have a lot?" queried Henry.

"Twenty or thirty," replied the Chinaman. "I am a photographic chemist."

The moment grew a fraction less oppressive. A photographic chemist—*not* a detective! While Henry was enjoying the information, the nymph was making use of it.

"Now listen, Mr. Photographic Chemist," she said, still retaining her note of severity. "You may be what you say, I'm not saying you're not, and you may have lost a camera, I'm not saying you haven't. But does that give you any right to walk up to anybody and say they've got the camera you've lost?"

"The proof is so simple," murmured the Chinaman.

"Oh, *is* it?" retorted the nymph. "I'm glad you think so! But what about *our* proof? Anybody can say, 'Ah, there's the dear old mark, that's mine!' "

The Chinaman turned to Henry and observed admiringly, "The way your friend keeps her end up!"

"Of course she keeps her end up," responded Henry. "She's that kind. So now answer her and let's see whether you can keep *your* end up!"

"Oh, quite simple," smiled the Chinaman. "No trouble at all. I haven't seen the camera yet, have I? Only enough, that is, to identify the make and the newness. So if I tell you that the mark is a simple little cross scratched in the north-west corner, so to speak, of the frame from which the lens and bellows emerge as you open the camera toward you—well, would that be enough?"

"Not if the camera was ours," retorted the nymph, her intelligence still working, "and even if it wasn't— for the sake of argument—we might want to know a bit more about it. So suppose you drop all this mystery business, young man, and give us something to bite on. Then p'r'aps we'll bite back!"

The Chinaman smiled.

"You win," he said. "And, after all, it's quite reasonable." He paused for an instant, then proceeded, "A man came into my shop this afternoon—common sort of fellow—and asked for a camera that would take photographs by artificial light. 'What sort of artificial light?' I said. 'Just an ordinary interior?' 'Well, say it was a fancy dress ball,' he said. 'Oh, you're going to the Chelsea Arts,' I said. 'Who said I was?' he snapped. 'Get on with it!' No, he didn't

say get, he said git. Nasty sort of chap. Well, I suggested he should use one of these."

He took from his pocket an object that made Henry
jump. The nymph nearly jumped also, but just managed to refrain. It was the odd-looking flashlight she
had rescued from the floor after the tussle earlier that
evening, and that had been snatched from Henry's
pocket later on. . . . The glass bulb at the end looked
different, though. . . .

"Whatever is it?" asked the nymph.

"Sashalite. Never seen one before?" inquired the
Chinaman. "They're rather good. You fix them onto
an ordinary electric torch by unscrewing the small
lamp with which the torch is ordinarily fitted, and
then screwing in this thing in its place. Fix your camera, open the shutter—so it will stay open—doesn't
matter in the artificial light—press the jigger on the
torch, and you get your flash. Picture's taken. Close
camera. There you are. Of course, this looks a mess
now because it's been used," he added, "but before
they are used they are prettier. Like an ordinary electric lamp stuffed with bright silver paper."

They recognized the description. The glass bulb
had looked like that when it had been in their possession.

"Now," continued the Chinaman, replacing the con-
trivance in his pocket, "my funny friend bought two

of these things. I don't know where the other is. . . .
No, my mistake, he didn't buy them. He didn't buy
anything. They were on the counter with the camera
and a roll of films, and I'd just turned my back to
add a camera-case he had suddenly asked for, when he
did a bunk."

"Oh, a thief," said the nymph.

"Yes. One of those fellows who like to get things
cheap. Of course he took the goods with him."

"Bad luck," said Henry.

"Yes—wasn't it. It made me ratty. And all at
once—just as I was about to go to bed, in fact—I wondered whether he really *was* going to the Chelsea Arts
Ball—he had seemed suspiciously upset by my suggestion—and whether he was going in for any crookedness there. The idea of catching him redhanded rather
appealed to me, especially as I have an Oriental costume in which I sometimes juggle at children's parties. Incidentally—one sees sights here. And pretty
ladies." He bowed to the nymph. "And so I came
along."

"Well, did you find the thief?" asked the nymph,
ignoring the bow.

"So far, all I've found is this," he said.

He produced the flashlight again.

"Yes, where did you find that?"

"I'll tell you. And also how. When I got here I

realized that I was looking for a needle in a haystack. In the first place, there must be thousands of people here—literally thousands. In the second, they were all dressed up. As I am. I was quite sure the thief would not recognize *me,* so I had little chance of recognizing him. But there was one fellow—dressed as a coster——" He paused, for Henry had drawn a quick breath. "You know him?"

"Go on," said the nymph quietly.

"I see—your friend has a toothache," murmured the Chinaman, with a smile. "Well, there was something about this coster that seemed vaguely familiar. I spoke to the woman he was with, and afterward had a word or two with him. Couldn't make up my mind, you know. Most attractive woman. Very superior to him. Dressed as some historical beauty, I believe——" He paused again. "Another twinge?" he asked Henry.

"You just *can't* tell a story right off, can you?" exclaimed the nymph. "What happened next? We can't sit here listening to you till breakfast!"

"Your friend happened next," the Chinaman answered her. "I'd decided to tackle the coster, had nearly caught him, and then had lost him. When I bumped into your friend a little while afterward— it was in the same vicinity—I thought it rather odd that he should have a camera in his pocket similar to

the one I was looking for. I made a remark. It appeared to upset him. He vanished."

"As a matter of fact, I wasn't feeling well," interposed Henry quickly. "I'd had more than usual to
drink."

"Yes, yes, I know the feeling," nodded the Chinaman. "And I didn't pay much attention to it. But
I've seen you once or twice since from a distance—
and you seemed so *very* unwell that it occurred to me
I might go back and explore the part of the hall where
I had lost the coster and found *you*. So I went back.
And I had a thorough search. I was just giving up
when I peeped into a nasty dark passage, and went
through into a nasty dark spot that appeared to be
nothing but steps. I stumbled down a few, till they
seemed to stop and shoot down into nowhere, and
then my foot kicked something. The torch I've shown
you."

He stopped speaking. Was he taking a breath, or
was that the end of the story?

"Find anything else?" asked the nymph.

"Not the camera," answered the Chinaman, his
eyes on Henry. "I thought *you* might have found
that—if you had come from the same spot?"

Then Henry answered a sane impulse and took the
camera from his pocket.

"Have a look," he said.

The Chinaman examined it, and nodded.

"Yes, it *is* mine," he said soberly.

"Well, I didn't steal it," replied Henry.

"I never said you did," returned the Chinaman, "and I never thought you did. You found it, of course?"

"Yes."

"Same place?"

"That's right."

"And missed the torch. Queer. But perhaps not. It mightn't have occurred to you to stay and see if anything else was knocking around, like I did."

"Oh! You stayed?"

"While my last match lasted. The torch was no use, of course, as it was spent, you only get one flash. I stayed to look for the camera."

"And didn't find it," interposed the nymph.

"Well, that's obvious."

"Or—anything else?"

"Anything else? What else would there be to find barring the thief himself, and he certainly wasn't there." His listeners tried hard not to look at each other, and failed. "You know, there's something you two are keeping back," went on the Chinaman, watching them. "I may find out what it is when I develop the spool—there's been one exposure—but I've an idea you could save me a lot of time."

Ignoring the nymph's frowns, Henry suddenly plunged.

"Yes—it's only fair to tell you," he blurted out. "You see, the fact is, I *did* find something else! I found your thief—and he was dead!"

The Chinaman blinked. Then he said politely:

"Do you mind repeating that?"

"Dead," muttered Henry.

The Chinaman should have looked shocked, but he merely looked incredulous.

"Is your friend well?" he asked, turning to the nymph.

"No, wonky!" she replied emphatically. "You've only got to look at him! It's true, what he said about his drinking. I believe his annual ration is one thimbleful, and a couple send him right off the reel. I expect he thought he'd been imagining things at first, and that's why he didn't report it. It's a fact he passed right out. And when I found him, I wouldn't let him report it. We've been sitting here arguing about it—and about you, because he thought you were chasing him—for God knows how long. Yes, and if I'd had my way, Mr. Photographic Chemist, you may as well know it, he wouldn't even have told *you*! If you've done a thing, stick it out, but if you haven't, let well alone—that's my motto!"

The Chinaman nodded.

"It's not a bad motto," he said thoughtfully. "Especially—well, after two thimblefuls."

"What's that mean?" demanded Henry.

"It means that you *may* have been imagining things," explained the Chinaman. "Dead men don't get up and walk away, you know."

Henry's brain began to reel again. The theory of imagination was almost as startling as the theory of reality. He recalled the ghastly moment and tried to convert it into a vision. He had undoubtedly been in a rum condition. And didn't drunken people sometimes see pink rats? . . .

"Yes, but what about the camera?" he exclaimed.

"Well, in your condition, the camera may have raised the ghost," suggested the Chinaman. "But that's not the only possibility. The fellow may have got into a scrap, been temporarily knocked out, and come to after you left him? Anyhow, we don't want to notify the police and then find we've made fools of ourselves. Wait here for me, will you?"

"Where are you going?" cried Henry, as the Chinaman jumped up.

"To have another look," answered the Chinaman, and darted away.

Henry clambered to his feet to follow him. He felt the nymph's fingers on his arm.

"No, you don't!" she said, and pulled him down again.

Mr. Shannon was alone once more. He sat in his box and watched the thinning crowd. It would be an hour before the floor was cleared of dancers and a new army took their place—an army of attendants and charwomen whose joyless job would be to wipe out frivolous memories with brooms and mops and water—but already there was a sense that limbs were flagging and minds were spent, and that people were flogging themselves to secure their full money's worth. Only half of them were dancing. The other half were sliding perilously, sometimes singly and sometimes in long processions, shouting senselessly, or smiling vacuously. One elderly man, the managing director of a company, was earnestly eying a large yellow balloon, one of the few that had failed to descend into the scrum. He had been eying it for a quarter of an hour, hoping it would come down softly and quietly so that he could secure it. He had tried to secure over a dozen other balloons, but had always failed to gain the prize. Once a man had hit him on the nose just as success was within his grasp. Another time he had hit a man on the nose. But he was quite certain he would not fail to get this yellow balloon, if only it descended. He would get it if every scrap of clothing were torn from his body. Why he wanted the balloon, or what he would do with it when he got it, were unimportant details. . . . Another man was strolling around singing serenades, accompanying himself on an imaginary guitar.

"Idiots!" thought Mr. Shannon.

Two of the idiots galloped by his box at that moment. They were his wife and his son.

He envied them.

Somebody knocked softly on the door. He did not hear the knock. His eyes were on another couple. They floated by, very close together. They seemed oblivious to everyone but themselves. The girl's eyes were half-closed. The man was obviously refraining from a primitive desire to kiss her. They were Mr. Shannon's daughter and Harold Lankester.

The soft knock was repeated.

"Eh? Come in!" called Mr. Shannon.

The door opened quietly, and the Balkan Prince stood in the doorway.

For a few seconds the two men regarded each other. They had never met face to face before, and beyond the fact that they had been born into the same world they had nothing in common. Their ideas, their reactions, their ambitions, their philosophies, were antipathetic. But Fate had thrown them together for this instant of time, and the instant had to be dealt with.

The Prince broke the silence with a remark that seemed trivial enough.

"Your daughter's handkerchief," he said. "She lost it when she danced with me."

"Thank you," answered Mr. Shannon.

The Prince advanced and held out the handkerchief. As Mr. Shannon took it, the Prince continued in a low voice:

"Many things get lost here. Have you, by chance, also lost a camera?"

Mr. Shannon did not reply. The separate pieces of a jig-saw, startled into violent kaleidoscopic activity, whirled round his mind and settled into a pattern.

"Or found one?" added the Prince.

Mr. Shannon swallowed slowly. Then he murmured:

"I see—I see! So—*that's* it!"

"You understand quickly," answered the Prince. "And that is well, because——"

"P'r'aps I understand a damn sight too quickly!" interrupted Mr. Shannon. "Have *you* lost a camera?"

"Somebody has lost a camera," replied the Prince, "but that somebody is no longer interested. He has ceased to be interested in any earthly thing."

"The devil!" thought Mr. Shannon.

The irony of the situation bit into him. He must bargain, after all, even though, had his visitor known it, he had nothing now to bargain with! And his visitor must not know it! There lay the humiliation. Mr. Shannon must make a pretense of yielding to blackmail.

"Well, say what you've come to say, and make it snappy!" he growled. "I'm listening."

"This is what I have come to say," responded the Prince, and his voice suddenly grew as edged as cold steel. "If you send any munitions out of the country in the next seven days you will be hanged for murder."

"You are, of course, a madman," remarked Mr. Shannon, after a pause, "but even madmen must be dealt with. So I am to be hanged for a murder I have not committed—is that it?"

"If you send those munitions you will commit a thousand murders. You will murder peaceful people, and bring tragedy into countless homes. But those are not the murders you will be hanged for. Such are permitted. To kill a worthless man, however— that is counted a sin."

"How about employing a worthless man?" countered Mr. Shannon, remembering too late that he was admitting facts by pursuing the argument in detail. "Is that a sin?"

The Prince shrugged his shoulders slightly.

"Not so long ago," he answered, "millions of men died fighting for peace. They did not have to pass moral examinations first. Nor did those who told them they were dying for peace——"

"Yes, yes, very interesting," interrupted Mr. Shannon nervously, and glanced out into the ballroom for an instant. This couldn't continue much longer. "But forgive me if I do not discuss moral questions with lunatics. Let us keep practical, for God's sake! Suppose—suppose I do *not* dispatch these munitions you talk of? What guarantee have I that you will not proceed with your lunacy?"

"You have my word."

"A promise from Colney Hatch!"

"And if I do not keep my word, why should you keep yours?"

"Well, that's true," admitted Mr. Shannon. "Yes—of course—— And the camera?"

"Ah, the camera." The Prince looked at Mr. Shannon searchingly. "You have not the camera, then?"

"That means *you* haven't!" replied Mr. Shannon sharply.

Confound it! But for his conversation with Harold Lankester and this new pressure that was being put upon him, he might have found some way of beating his opponent yet!

"It means that neither of us has," said the Prince. "But if I had it, it would now be of no use, since I would not use it. I have, as you call it, a stronger card. And if you had it, it might be an awkward possession."

"You are full of information!"

"May I ask, did you touch the camera?"

"May I ask, why the devil do you want to know?"

"It will be better for you if there are no finger-prints."

"I am obliged to you, sir, for your solicitation! No, I did not touch it." Sudden horror entered his face, driving away its sarcasm. "But *somebody's* got it!"

"Yes, that is unfortunate. It is the slight risk, for you, that remains. But perhaps, after all, it is only slight. You and I, at least, have no need to fear each other any more. That is so?"

"Eh? Oh, yes, yes, that's so. But how about your accomplices? What about *them*?"

"One is dead."

"But the other. Yes, by God, p'r'aps *she's* got the damned thing——"

"She has not got the camera," interposed the Prince. "And if she had, she would destroy its contents."

"Yes—I see," murmured Mr. Shannon. "You mean they might incriminate her also?"

"That is only a part of my meaning," responded the Prince, with a faint smile.

"What's the other part?"

"I have spoken with her since you saw her yourself, and I have formed the conclusion that, for a lady of her kind, she has too many scruples."

The heavy situation became momentarily a little brighter, although it was a hopeless sort of illumination that made Mr. Shannon's eyes suddenly glow for an instant.

"Are you telling me she's sorry?" he demanded.

"I am certain of it," replied the Prince.

He turned toward the door, and as he did so, it burst open. Conrad bounced in, stopped suddenly, and grinned.

"Aha! I'm right, Sis!" he cried over his shoulder. "He's brought your handkerchief!" But then his grin vanished and he looked puzzled. "Yes, but that's a funny thing! How've you got here so quickly? Didn't I see you on the other side of the hall a minute ago trying to catch a Dago in a black cloak? . . . Good Lord—he's gone!"

The Prince had told Sally to go home. She had completed her job, or as much of it as was possible, and all that remained as far as she was concerned was to return and await her pay. Even the necessity of passing on a portion of that pay to her accomplice had been gruesomely removed. But she had never regarded this commission in a mercenary light, and she found it impossible to leave the hall with so many other issues undecided.

What would be the outcome of the interview between her employer and her victim? The fact that this was not her concern did not eliminate her necessity to know the result. When would her accomplice's body be found, and what would be the interpretation of those who found it? This was her concern, as were the questions—where was the camera, and into whose hands had it fallen? If the camera fell into the hands of the police and were traced to Sam, the spool of films would probably be developed with disastrous results. That flashlight photograph would be a scoop for the detectives and the journalists!

"Yes, I've *got* to find the camera!" she thought. "Somehow or other!"

The thought turned her steps in the direction of the spot where she had last seen it. Perhaps it was still knocking around there, in some odd corner. It might have fallen into the dark well before Sam's own body had followed it. Her mind remained undecided while she walked. She was not sure whether she possessed sufficient courage to return again to that black hell. But her feet ignored her mental indecision, and carried her on. . . .

"Good-evening!"

She managed not to jump. It was the Chinaman.

"Good-evening," she answered, coolly. "Do I know you?"

"We met once before," he reminded her.

"I'm afraid I don't remember," she replied.

"You have less cause to than I!" he sighed, rather fatuously. "A Chinaman makes no impression, but beauty——"

"Yes, thank you, but it's a bit too late for compliments, the varnish has worn off," she interrupted. "And, now I look at you, I do remember you. You haven't lost your ivy manner."

"Ivy?"

"It clings, doesn't it? Well, as before, I'm not in a clinging mood, so——"

She stopped abruptly. The Chinaman had raised a protesting hand, and a capacious blue sleeve had flowed back a little from the fingers it had all but concealed. The fingers were clasping a camera.

"So what?" asked the Chinaman.

Sally's eyes were not on the camera when she answered him. If it held any interest for her, she was astute enough not to show it.

"Nothing, Mr. Wu," she yawned. "I believe I was going to be rude, but you must forgive me, I'm tired. Was there anything particular you wanted to say?"

"Oh, no," answered the Chinaman casually. "I hope you found your friend, that's all."

"Friend? What friend?" demanded Sally, covering

her palpitations with a frown. "I thought it was *you* who were waiting for someone?"

"Ah, your memory is improving!" smiled the Chinaman. "Yes, I was. I had an idea you were, too. A man dressed as a coster I'd seen you with before."

"He *does* know something—how much?" thought Sally rapidly, and her interest in the camera doubled. Aloud she said, "Coster? Oh, yes—early in the evening. But one could hardly describe him as a friend."

"No?"

"He picked me up—and then I dropped him. You may have gathered yourself that I don't like being picked up."

"I have gathered it," replied the Chinaman.

He looked at her solemnly. Her story seemed a very probable one. People did pick each other up at public balls. . . .

"Then you're not interested in him?" he inquired.

"My dear man, why should I be?" she retorted, with wide, innocent eyes. "Are you? If you know anything about him, perhaps you had better put me wise, in case I bump into him again. I had a hope he had gone home!"

She wanted to scream in the little silence that preceded his answer, but her eyes remained serene and innocent. They gave no indication of their owner's mood.

"Well, as a matter of fact, I don't really know anything about him either," said the Chinaman, "but he seemed pretty drunk when I came across him, and so I'm glad for your sake, that he *isn't* a friend. I hope he wasn't in that condition when he danced with you?"

"Drunk as a lord," declared Sally, "so you can imagine I dropped him early!"

"Disgraceful! Personally, I've no use for drinking—save medicinally. Still, ideas differ. He struck me as the kind of chap who could get himself right bowled over—creep away somewhere to sleep it off—and then crawl home after the milkman. That your impression? Or should I be hauled up for slander?"

"It's distinctly my impression," said Sally. "But—if one may ask—what made you develop yours to that extent?"

The Chinaman laughed. He seemed suddenly rather pleased with life.

"To be perfectly truthful, I'm a little more interested in that fellow than I've pretended," he said confidentially, "and I'm clearing up a minor mystery. There's a man here—probably an Edgar Wallace fan—who thinks he has seen the fellow's corpse! Don't be alarmed. I imagine the Edgar Wallace fan has been drinking pretty steadily himself, and it's a curious fact that one drunken man never recognizes another—he assumes something worse. Anyhow, as *I'd* also been in the spot where the alleged corpse lay and hadn't seen anything, I put two and two together, and I'm just on my way to prove that they make four. I may say my conversation with you has confirmed my theory."

"The theory being——"

"Haven't I told you? That—if my friend saw anything at all—the dead man he saw wasn't dead but drunk, and has crawled home."

"I see," said Sally slowly. "Well, if I've confirmed the theory I should let the matter drop, and crawl home yourself."

"No, no—I do things thoroughly," replied the Chinaman. "Oh, by the way, I don't suppose the fellow took your photograph?"

"Why should he have?" asked Sally sharply.

"What? I'm sorry," answered the Chinaman, pulled up by her tone. "I meant without permission, of course. You see, he had a camera. Here it is. He evidently dropped it."

"Then how did you get hold of it?" inquired Sally, grateful for the opportunity of putting a question she had longed to put before.

"It was returned to me by my rather morbid friend."

"*Returned* to you——?"

"Even so, madame. It is mine. Our rascally coster

stole it from my shop only this afternoon—no, I am wrong—yesterday afternoon—and as he also stole a roll of films and a flashlight, and had previously mentioned a fancy dress ball, I concluded his object was to snap Venuses. That was why I asked whether he had snapped you. How mysterious everything is when you don't know it, and how simple when you do!"

Sally's mind had raced many times that evening, but never faster than it was racing now. The camera was in the Chinaman's hand. A quick snatch, and it could be in hers. Sally had snatched things before. . . .

"Well, I mustn't keep you any longer," said the Chinaman, preparing to depart. "If I fail to find my man—and, to let you into another secret, he's the only reason for my being here at all—I've found the goods, and when I develop the film it will be interesting to see who he *has* taken."

To the Chinaman's surprise he found the attractive lady's hand upon his arm.

"I'd leave matters where they are, if I were you," she said. "If that drunken fellow *is* still lying about, you'll only get into trouble."

"Oh, no—*he'll* get into trouble," replied the Chinaman.

"Why let anybody get into trouble?" she asked. "The party's nearly over. Let's dance it out?"

She gave him a provocative smile, although she did

not feel in the least provocative. She seemed a very different creature now from the cold individual of their original meeting. The Chinaman, ignorant of the cause, was conscious of the change.

But he hesitated for only a second or two.

"No, no," he exclaimed. "You said you were tired and didn't like people who tried to pick you up. This is just kindness. I won't take advantage of it. I'll finish my job, reassure my anxious friend, and then go home. Good-night!"

He turned away with a quick smile. "Damn him!" thought Sally. "Idiot I was!" thought the Chinaman. He was really keen on finishing his job, but he had a depressing sensation that he had missed the chance of a lifetime.

He continued on his way. He was not far from his destination. A short curve brought him to a point from where he could see the shadow of the passage. He hurried forward, with a sudden desire to get it over.

Now he was in the passage. Now he was through it, and in the dark, uncharted space. Dash! He had no more matches. How the deuce was he to search this place without any light? Well, he would have to grope about, and perhaps, if he did it systematically. . . .

He tripped on a stair, and just saved himself from

falling. In saving himself, he all but lost the camera. He placed it on the ground, marking the spot. If there were any more trips he wanted both hands free. Besides . . .

Besides what? He refused to admit it at first. Then, raising his head sharply, he did admit it. It was a nasty sensation that he was not alone. He could not be *sure* that he had just heard a soft sound, or that, a few seconds earlier, a vague form had flitted in and out of the corner of his eye. This certainly was a spot for imagination, all right! But he was very nearly sure.

"Anybody there?" he called.

If there was, the person betrayed no disposition to reveal himself.

The Chinaman continued to grope about unsatisfactorily. He felt rather like the blind man who was sent to search in a dark room for a black cat that was not there. The coster—dead, drunk, or sober—seemed as absent as the cat. Unless, of course, that shadow over there. . . . What shadow? It was gone.

"I'm seeing things," decided the Chinaman. "I'll chuck it, and report all clear. And then—why not?— I'll try and find something more appealing than a corpse—that attractive lady. If she's still in the mood, I think I've earned my dance!"

He turned and felt his way back to the spot where

he had left the camera. He knew it exactly. He had a good bump of geography. But when he stooped, his hand met empty floor.

"Well, I'm dashed!" he muttered. "I could have sworn——"

He moved to another spot. Then to another. Annoyance, dismay, and uneasiness contended against one another as he moved about, and twice he turned swiftly with a nasty feeling that somebody was immediately behind him. But in each case he stared into nothingness.

"This is ridiculous!" he told himself. "Confound it all! *I* haven't been drinking!"

He was quite certain that he had not made a mistake in the spot where he had left the camera. Another person would have derided his certainty, but that made no difference. Sometimes you are sure of a thing even though you cannot explain why, and the Chinaman was sure of this. He was also sure that his hand had not missed the camera as it had groped about. Still, he returned to the spot, for another hopeless search. . . .

His hand touched something.

"Whew!" he muttered.

The camera was there!

He stood, considering. He struggled to convince

himself that he had been mistaken, after all, and the fact that he could not convince himself made the place doubly uncanny. He imagined footsteps. He imagined whispers. He knew, this time, that he was imagining. But he did not know that something was shortly to happen within a few feet of where he stood that was far beyond anything he could imagine. . . .

"What am I standing here for?" he suddenly asked himself. "What am I waiting for?"

He had got his camera. He had searched diligently and dutifully, and fruitlessly for the alleged corpse. True, he had not descended into the most precipitous part where the long, seatlike steps appeared to fall away into a bottomless pit, but he did not see why he should risk a sprained ankle, or that the risk held out any prospects of success. It was fairly obvious that the fuddled fellow whose hallucination the China- man was proving had not come upon his vision down in the pit, or he would never in his condition have got up again. This logic may have been faulty, but the Chinaman was not in a mood to examine it search- ingly. He wanted to go, and to forget gloomy things in the brightness of a lady's eyes.

But, when he was outside, he did not find the lady, though he made a complete search of the thinning throngs.

At the beginning of the Chelsea Arts Ball, you will have no chance of slipping by the lynx-eyed officials and securing your entertainment for nothing. You may ascend the few wide steps to the entrance, but you will soon be descending them again if you cannot show your ticket. Gate-crashers find it easier to attend parties where there is no entrance fee. But toward the end of the evening, or more correctly speaking the beginning of the morning, the official eye has grown a little sleepy, and you may encounter it when it is inattentive. This fact assisted two people to join in the final flicker of the ball without any right to do so.

Each had to adopt a little ruse, however. The first, who arrived outside the hall some while before the second, paused for a few moments until there was a little crush in the doorway. Then, quickly, he joined it. He had nearly pushed his way in when an official vaguely barred his way.

"Please! I have my taxi, it will not wait!" snapped the gate-crasher. "My friends—they are inside—I must tell them to hurry!"

The official melted away. He was not really interested. And he did not know that the black-coated gentleman with a slight foreign accent who had just spoken to him had a dagger in his pocket.

The second gate-crasher was very different. Earlier in the evening he had been an imposing figure, and

would have commanded respect. Now his glory had
departed. His splendid clothes were creased and
stained, even torn in places. His cheeks were pale.
His breath came in tragic gasps. But he, too, had the
sense to wait for a few moments in order to collect
himself a little before he walked unsteadily up the
steps to the entrance.

"Hallo! Somebody's had a gay time!" laughed a
young man in his face.

"A bit too gay," reflected the official, stifling a
yawn. Not that excess of gaiety was a matter for comment. The official's ideas of life had broadened considerably during the past half-dozen hours. Responding to a vague sense of duty, possibly inspired by the
return of a policeman who had just assisted an in-
ebriate Viking off the premises, he intruded himself
in the path of the bedraggled newcomer and said,
"No pass-out checks, sir. You're not supposed to come
in again, once you've been out."

"I've got to come in," muttered the newcomer.

"Oh, have you?" frowned the official.

"Yes, I have," answered the newcomer, and suddenly made a pathetic attempt to be authoritative.
"I am Warwick Hilling—the actor."

"Ah!" said the official. Warwick Hilling? Never
heard of him! But perhaps he ought to have—and,
now he came to think of it, he did believe he had seen

a chap togged up something like this. Only then, of
course, he hadn't looked as though he had been
thrown up by a volcano. . . .

Hallo! The fellow had dived by! Given him a
push, too! The official turned to follow him, then
stopped and shrugged his shoulders.

"What's it matter?" he smiled to the policeman.
"It'll be all the same a hundred years hence!"

The policeman did not respond. His eyes were following the disappearing figure. Slowly he trudged in
its wake. It looked rather like another spot of trouble,
but he wasn't going to hurry to overtake it.

It is doubtful whether the policeman could have
overtaken it even if he had hurried, for Warwick Hilling had lost his self-confidence as well as his judgment,
and the panic that had caused his abrupt and unwise
rush continued for a full minute. In that space of
time he covered a considerable distance, and amused
or startled a number of people. These people were of
no importance to him provided they merely stood and
stared, and did not interfere with his object of placing
as great a distance as possible between himself and
the entrance, but one man with the hunting instinct
did give a "Huick-holler!" and set chase. Hilling
did not shake him off until he had traveled round an
appreciable length of the hall's vast circle and had
ascended to the second tier. Then he spied the open

door of an empty box. He dived in, like a hunted fox, closed the door, and sank into a chair.

The huntsman ran by, and lost the scent.

The box proved a godsend. Its original occupants had long gone home, and nobody disturbed him. Recovering gradually, Hilling began to take a slightly more intelligent interest in his surroundings, but complete intelligence could not be his until he had had twelve hours of solid undisturbed sleep. His brain seemed finally to have given up its struggle from the moment he had burned his boats and struck the constable in the foggy street, and how he had subsequently muddled his way from that point to this was a mystery which Hilling himself could never explain. Had he asked the way of an old woman in a doorstep? He couldn't be sure. Had he passed an uneasy period at a coffee-stall? It might be. Had he managed a short spell in a taxi? He couldn't remember. Everything was vague, and strange, and inexplicable. . . . But here he was! And below him was a scene that was equally vague and strange and inexplicable. Balloons. Haze. Lights. Music. People dancing. People sliding. People careering about. Yes, and somewhere among all these people were two with whom he, Warwick Hilling, was vitally concerned. "Oh, nonsense!" thought Hilling. "That can't be. I'm not *really* here."

"You *are* really here!" he told himself the next

moment. "Stick to it! You know you're really here, and you are only trying to fool yourself because you are tired!" God, he was tired!

He opened his eyes suddenly. Had he been asleep? Damn all these unanswerable questions! Wasn't he ever to know anything again, not even about his own personal actions? "Heavens above!" he thought. "I've even forgotten why I'm here!" His eyes closed again. He forced his fingers into them and opened them. "Now, why am I here?" he asked aloud. "It'll come in a minute. You've been drugged, you know. Why was I drugged? It'll come in a minute!"

He waited for it to come. He knew how to do it. Just make your mind a perfect blank—that was easy—and then a picture would appear. It would develop suddenly on the negative of the mind. . . . The negative of the mind. Rather a good expression, that. Was it his—or Shakespeare's? . . .

But it did not come suddenly. It came softly, and slowly. And it began with a slight, a very slight creak.

"Ah!" thought Hilling, vapidly. "A creak. Something about a creak——"

Now another soft sound, as of a handle turning. Creak. Handle turning. They didn't make sense. He must wait a moment longer, and keep very still, and then . . . Ah! Footsteps. Now we're getting somewhere. —Creak—handle turning—footstep—footstep!

And then knowledge pierced the numbness of Hilling's comprehension with a swift, burning pain. This wasn't happening in his mind, it was happening in reality, behind him.

"Ah!" he shouted, and swung round.

He saw two eyes. They stared at him from beneath a sweating forehead. He also saw the gleam of a knife. But the knife was as motionless as the eyes. For the eyes were transfixed with a desperate, almost terrified recognition, and as they recognized Hilling, so he recognized them. The last time he had seen them he had been bound down on a table.

Suddenly the assassin turned and vanished. But Hilling was after him. Across the passage . . .

"There's that fellow again!" called a voice in the distance. "Huick! Huick!"

The huntsman did not set chase this time, however. He had been caught himself, by his wife, and his arm was in the grip of her firm, determined fingers.

Through an opening. Down a staircase. Vague voices about him. . . .

"Personally, my opinion is that the whole thing's sheer lunacy!"

"Oh, I don't know. It does people good to let off steam sometimes."

Down another staircase. . . .

"No, don't interfere. It's only a game."

Along a corridor. Into a youth dressed in gold. Along another corridor. Through a gap. Into a chain of gallopers. . . .

"Go it, Near East!"

"What's this? Training for the Olympic Sports?"

"Come along! Join in! Right round the hall this time!"

Hilling's hand was seized by one of the gallopers. "Let go!" he gasped.

"No, the other chap's gone, and we want you!" cried the galloper. "The more the merrier. Atta boy!"

Humanity swarmed around him. He became imprisoned in a living, whirling mass. For a while there was no escape from it. "Cheer up!" giggled a girl in his face. She was not pretty, but her utter abandon to the moment gave her a certain primitive charm. "The worst is yet to come!" Hilling doubted it. Could worse exist?

The revolving mass broke, re-formed, broke again, re-formed again. Near its center personal volition ceased to exist, and one began to understand the principle of the Solar System. But the Solar System has billions of years of tradition behind it, and the system of this lesser mass had none. It was a momentary, an ephemeral evolution, formed of conflicting particles that were bound together by no permanent unity, and its center changed as its bulk and formation shifted.

Presently release came to the particular particle in which we are interested. The pressure behind Hilling's back took a new direction. He felt himself being squeezed toward the outer circumference. The final expulsion shot him into an onlooker's arms.

The onlooker, though Hilling did not know it, had stationed himself especially to receive him, and led the limp form away. All at once the Universe ceased to whirl and became very quiet. Hilling looked up, and found himself staring at his double.

"Recover yourself," said his double, in a smooth, low voice. "Then we will talk."

"Are you—are you——?" panted Hilling.

"Yes," answered the Prince. "You and I have met before this evening. But take your time. Unless—there is no time?"

Hilling gulped. The Prince gathered that there was no time, for Hilling's complete collapse looked imminent. He allowed a few seconds to pass, then asked:

"What has happened? Can you tell me?"

"Must tell you—quickly——!" spluttered Hilling.

But as the spluttering ceased, the Prince realized that he must assist in the telling. He recalled a dying

soldier from whom he had once extracted vital information in the last available minute. He now adopted
similar tactics, although Hilling was not dying.

"Just answer briefly. My friend drove you to my
house?" Hilling nodded.

"And you both waited there?"

Hilling nodded again.

"But—there was trouble?"

"Shot at!" gasped Hilling.

If the information surprised the Prince, he did not
show it. He repeated quietly:

"Shot at. The ruse was successful, then, beyond expectation. But—they missed?"

"No. Yes. Then. I'll tell you . . . my head . . ."

"Then?" said the Prince. "They missed—*then?*"
And suddenly he asked sharply, "Where is my
friend?"

"Eh?" muttered Hilling. "Yes, I—I was just about
to—I'm afraid———"

"They got him?"

Hilling nodded. The Prince swung his head away.
In his line of vision stood a woman. He did not see
her, but she saw him, and later she tried to describe
his expression to her husband. "Do you know, it
really frightened me," she said, "though I only saw
it for a moment. . . ."

The Prince turned back to Hilling. The expression

had come and gone, but it had left its mark. There was something terrible in his eyes. They glinted with controlled white heat.

"How?" he asked. "A bullet?"

"No. Gas, I think," replied Hilling. "Not—sure."

After a pause:

"But you escaped?"

"Somehow."

"Yes? And then?"

"They caught me." In a sudden nausea of emotion, he grabbed the Prince's arm. "Devils—they're devils! They caught me and drugged me! Bound me! Tried to kill me! Yes, yes, and now one of them's come here and tried again—with a knife—thinking I was you! He's after you—that's why I'm here—he's after you——"

The words came in spasmodic, weeping gasps. Now, abruptly, they ceased, and the fingers loosened on the Prince's sleeve. An attendant strolled along, and paused.

"My twin brother is not well," said the Prince.

"Ah," answered the attendant, understandingly.

"Do you think we could get him to a couch?" asked the Prince.

"He won't be the first," replied the attendant. "But I suggest you get him home, sir. We'll all be shifting in a few minutes."

"It is those few minutes he needs," returned the Prince. "And I need them, too, for I have something to do here before I go. Could you watch him for me until I come back for him, and see he comes to no harm?"

The attendant looked a little doubtful.

"Well, I'm not sure——" he began. A pound note was slipped into his hand. "Don't worry, sir," smiled the attendant. "I'll keep my eye on him!"

They got him to a couch. Then the Prince slipped away.

You would not have known if you had passed the Prince that he had a care in the world. His attitude was untroubled as he made a leisurely tour of the hall. Above all, it would never have occurred to you that he knew he was being tracked by a man with a knife, for he made no attempt to conceal himself, and seemed indeed to delight in making himself as conspicuous as possible. But the Prince had eyes at the back of his head, and he noticed all who noticed him.

He strolled three times in each direction round the complete horseshoe of the ground-floor corridor. He made several deliberate excursions onto the dancing floor itself, often pausing to watch the revelers from the prominence of empty spaces. Then he ascended to the higher corridors, and strolled along those. Now he

passed fewer people. He came to a corridor where the
population was reduced to three. Farther along the
corridor there was nobody, but he paused before entering that No Man's Land.`

One of the three people within his range of vision
was a Chinaman. The Chinaman was walking fast, or
the Prince would have addressed him, and the course
of the next five minutes would have been altered. But
the Chinaman was in a hurry, and the Prince chose
the other two for his inquiry. The other two wore
red uniforms, and rather resembled musical comedy
generals. They looked thoroughly incapable of winning a war.

"Pardon me," said the Prince politely. "I wonder
whether you could direct me to a spot I am looking
for. I am sure it is about here somewhere."

He spoke loudly. Somebody lurking not far behind
him listened intently.

"Spot? What spot?" replied one of the generals.

"Spot barred?" added the other, and they both
laughed as at some mighty jest.

"I am afraid it is not easy to describe," answered
the Prince. "You approach it through a narrow passage. An empty, dark place——"

"Empty and dark?" said the first general.

"Now, do you know, sir," smiled the second, "that
sounds just like the inside of my head!"

And he laughed again, while the first general inquired:

"Is it wise to seek dark and empty spots at this time of night?"

"I came upon it by accident," explained the Prince, "and I am only returning to it now because I dropped something there. But for that, I should agree with you. It is a perfect place for a stumble. . . . Ah!" he cried suddenly. "Just ahead there—now I know where I am. Forgive me for having troubled you. Good-evening."

He left them abruptly.

"Queer fellow," commented the first general.

"Everything's queer," said the second general. "You're queer. I'm queer. Come on!"

They continued on their way, and were so absorbed in the queerness of things that they did not notice a man who suddenly slipped by them. The man who had overheard the conversation.

A few seconds later, the Prince was in the narrow passage. He groped his way into the dark region beyond. He paused for an instant, listening, but his pose gave no clue to his attentiveness. Then he moved again, feeling his way along the unevenly terraced ground.

Someone moved behind him. As the Prince descended, taking a zigzag course, toward the spot where earlier the coster had lain, the distance between himself and his follower lessened. The follower walked softly, but the Prince made no attempt to be silent.

Presently the Prince paused.

"That is strange," he said aloud. "I thought I dropped it here."

He stooped, groping. The man behind him drew closer still. Now five yards separated them. Now three.

"I wonder whether this is the place, after all?" communed the Prince, still thinking aloud. "Yes, I feel sure. Perhaps a little more to the left——"

He moved to the left. So did the man behind him. Now only two yards separated them. Now one. A dagger gleamed palely, raised suddenly high.

It remained raised. The prince had swung round with the litheness of a panther, seizing the hand that held the dagger. If the woman who had been frightened by the Prince's expression in the hall below had seen his expression now, she would have screamed. But the only person who saw it did not scream. He stood galvanized. And he only saw it because it was within a few inches of his bulging eyes.

"Devil!" hissed the Prince. "Devil! Devil!"

The dagger slid to the ground, squeezed out by ruthless fingers. It made a hideous little clatter. Then

296 DEATH IN FANCY DRESS

the assassin was lifted higher than the dagger had been and was hurled through the blackness. He fell, with a broken neck, within a foot of where the coster lay.

The Prince stood very still. He had seen many dead men, but this was the first he had killed. His conscience was clear, for his philosophy was only halfway toward the pacifism he believed in. And how few of us have freed ourselves from the axiom that the end justifies the means, and have learned that the means we employ form the only end we can be sure of? But vengeance also lay behind the Prince's act— vengeance for the death of a friend. Though he disliked his act, he would have performed it again.

He stooped, and picked up the dagger. He picked it up by its point, and threw it after its owner. Then something rustled behind him, and he turned. A woman stared at him, dazed.

"How long have you been here?" he asked, harshly.

"All the while," she whispered.

"Then—you saw?"

"Only the end. I was hiding—I didn't know till— and when it all happened——"

She stopped and shuddered violently. She was finding speech difficult.

After a pause the Prince said, with a little shrug, "It was just—it had to be. He would have killed me, and has already killed a man I loved. In this way, sometimes, events must happen." His voice was stern. There was no apology in it. But now it took on a more gentle tone as he continued, "But I do not understand. Did you follow me?"

"No."

"Then how are you here?"

"I came here before you."

"Why?"

"For—this!"

She held up a spool of films. He regarded it for a moment uncomprehendingly. Then, suddenly, intelligence dawned, and he smiled.

"Then nothing is now left undone," he said. "Yes, my friend judged you well. You are clever. But we will talk later. Now we must go. No, not together— I first. Count ten slowly after I have gone, and if I do not return, you will know the coast is clear."

He moved, but she seized his arm.

"What—about *them?*" she whispered.

"I think they have killed each other in a quarrel," answered the Prince. "How foolish these hotheads are—and how well the world is rid of them."

The next moment he was gone.

FIVE A.M.

"WELL, thank God *that's* over!" exclaimed the nymph, as the taxi bore them eastward.

The remark depressed Henry. He, too, felt that he could not have stood much more of it. His head ached, and his mind felt empty, and his personality, so strangely buoyant during the earlier hours of the ball, had been drained out of him. He had nothing more to give, and hardly any capacity left to receive. Even the fact that the nymph's knee jogged against his as the taxi turned or swerved meant little to him now. And if this was all, wasn't life meaningless? And didn't the future loom uninvitingly, with its new tantalizing memories that led nowhere? Still . . .

"Didn't you enjoy it, then?" he asked.

"Oh, yes, I enjoyed it," replied the nymph, "but even things you enjoy are sometimes best when they're done with. You can have too much of a good thing. And some of it wasn't too good, was it?" She glanced at him solemnly, then giggled at his expression. "Cheer up, Gauguin! By the way, what's your Sun-

298

day-go-to-meeting name? Time we shed our glory!"

"Henry Brown," he replied, trying hard not to be ashamed of it.

"Henry Brown," she repeated, making it sound a little nicer. "Well, Henry Brown, don't you want to know mine?"

"Of course I do—I was going to ask you," he said. "I know your address—you gave it to the taximan."

"I'm sorry I can't say Evelyn Laye or Tallulah Bankhead," answered the nymph. "It's Elsie Martin. But I didn't choose it, so it'll have to do. And, while we're at it, I work in a shop. Good-by, dreams!"

"What's wrong with a shop?" demanded Henry. "People have got to buy things, haven't they?"

"Three cheers for the red, white and blue!" laughed Elsie Martin. "And many thanks for defending my profession. But I may as well tell you, Mr. Henry Brown, that my shop days may be over. See, a friend of mine wants me to come in with her and give dancing lessons."

"My hat, you could do that all right!"

"Yes, *you'd* think so, because you'd only danced with ha'penny-hoppers before you danced with me——"

"That's true."

"There you are! Just the same, my friend thinks

I've got the gift, so I may make good at it. Will you be my first pupil?"

"You bet!" exclaimed Henry. "That is—I mean, yes, you bet!"

"Oh, Henry Brown, you are the most *transparent* thing!" she cried, poking him. "One can see through you plainer than a thin dress on a sunny day! What you meant was, 'If I can afford it!' Well, you can come off your high horse with me, *I* know you're not Rockefeller! I won't charge you anything. You'll be good to practice on!"

Was she serious? Or was she just making conversation because he himself hadn't any? How she kept up this tongue-rattle amazed Henry. He admired her for it—well, rather!—but all *he* could do was to lie back and answer her questions. He felt somehow that he wanted to be quiet. He didn't know why. . . .

Presently she sensed his need, or found the effort of doing all the work beyond her. They lapsed into a silence. Several times she looked at him oddly—half-solemn, half-amused—and smiled at the little space between them.

"My God, he's good!" she thought. "How does he live?"

But she did not break the silence till near the end of the journey. Then, recognizing local streets, she said:

"Well, we're nearly there. Anything you want to
say?"

"Eh?" jerked Henry.

"Oh, nothing," she murmured.

He roused himself.

"I'm awfully sorry—I'm afraid I've been very boring," he apologized. "The fact is, I—I was thinking."

"Can I have the thought for a penny?"

"I was thinking about that—you know—that coster
chap." She sighed to herself. "Do you suppose it
really was all my imagination? I mean, no nonsense.
Really?"

"Mr. Wu told us he wasn't there."

"Yes, I know he did."

"And I'm quite certain he was speaking the truth.
And I'm quite certain, too, that you've seen a *lot* of
things tonight that weren't there. So why not this
one?"

Henry nodded.

"I dare say," he said. "Yes, I dare say. But it's
funny." Then suddenly he burst out, "Do you know,
this time yesterday I'd never felt a *thing*—not properly—and now I've been up at the top and down to
the bottom!"

The nymph smiled. She had experienced a reflection of Henry's shock herself, but she knew there were
greater depths than the mere sight of a dead man,

real or imagined, and greater heights than a dance with a pretty girl.

"I suppose one's bound to feel a bit depressed," murmured Henry.

"Don't you know even *yet* what's worrying you?" exclaimed the nymph. "My God! See if kissing me will remove the depression! . . ."

"Hell!" muttered Henry, a few moments later. "The damn thing's stopping! . . ."

Ten minutes after that, it stopped again; this time before Henry's house. He alighted with exaggerated nonchalance, and his expression while he paid his fare was intended to convey the impression that he was thoroughly bored with existence; but his heart was thumping violently and his soul was whirling wildly with new experience, and the taximan knew all about it.

When he had crept up the long, steep staircases that led to his humble castle and quietly opened his bedroom door, he was astonished to find the room exactly as he had left it, though he would have been more astonished if he had found it filled with appropriate roses. The slightly rumpled bed, the chair, the hairbrush, the boots, one on its side, the little mirror. . . .

He crossed to the mirror and stared in it.

"You know, you wouldn't *think* it," he said

earnestly to his reflection. "But, well, there must be *something* in me. I mean—mustn't there?"

"Wasn't it fun?" yawned Mrs. Shannon, as she struggled out of her china shepherdess costume.

"Eh? Yes. Very much," answered Mr. Shannon abstractedly.

His mind being elsewhere, he was only vaguely conscious that the reply was not quite satisfactory. But as Mrs. Shannon was not conscious of it, either, it did not matter. At 5:00 A.M. one is not particular.

"And didn't Dorothy look lovely?" continued Mrs. Shannon. "Much better than last year. You know, I always hated that Fatima costume, though of course I didn't tell her. This was much prettier."

"Quite," agreed Mr. Shannon, removing his wig.

"Oh, well, the children enjoyed themselves, anyway," said Mrs. Shannon, revealing the real truth about her own feelings without intending to.

"I should hope they did—it cost enough!" retorted Mr. Shannon. "But didn't *you* enjoy it, too?"

It ought to have been a kindly inquiry, but it came more in the nature of a challenge.

"Yes, naturally! Didn't I say so?" The challenge flustered her a little. "I'm sure it does one good— once in a while. But, of course, it's really an occasion for young people, isn't it——"

"And we're old and decrepit," interposed Mr.
Shannon. "The breadwinner and the housekeeper.
Exactly."

He did feel ashamed of himself that time as he pretended not to notice the rather hurt look his wife
shot at him, but he was all on edge, and in the con-
ventional security of their bedroom—the dull, dull
safety of it—he was suffering from reaction. He
wanted to be alone for a week. After that he could
face his wife with understanding and even affection
for the rest of their lives. Yes, he was sure of that.
Especially as there might not be so very much more
of their lives. But just at this moment . . . Not very
much more of their lives? Well, of their vital interest in life, anyway! Wasn't that just the whole devil
of the business? Before long, perhaps, one or other of
them would be struck down . . . and then, the pain
of the one, and the remorse of the other! It didn't
bear thinking about. No, one mustn't think about
it. But if only the vital interest would end, meanwhile! It wasn't fair that it had ended for her, and
not for him! . . .

Had it ended for her? The sudden wonder made
Mr. Shannon pause in the operation of removing a
red-heeled shoe. It swept over him, with a sense of
terrible discovery, that he didn't know anything about
his wife. He hadn't known anything for years. Was

she equally ignorant of him? "Thank God, I've got my work!" he reflected.

She hadn't.

"I thought Harold was rather quiet," said Mrs. Shannon.

Yes—Harold, by Jove! Harold had delivered that bombshell! But maybe the bombshell would prove a blessing in disguise. If Mr. Shannon had been *forced* into relinquishing this contract, there would have been nothing but loss and · humiliation in it. Now, at least, the loss would be minimized, and the gain . . . Sir Henry Shannon! Sir Henry and Lady Shannon . . . might even be a "Bart." after it! After all, damn it, this was a pretty big thing he was doing for his country! And for the peace of the world! For a moment Henry Shannon really thought it was, since justification and self-esteem were second nature to him. Then the vision of a dead man rose in his mind, and wiped out the big thing. . . . No, no, not dead. Just knocked out. These drunken curs could lie like a log for a week. Why, now he came to think of it, he believed he had read a story once in which a drunken chap. . . . His wife had said something. Had he answered her?

"Yes, he was," answered Henry Shannon.

"I wonder if there was a special reason, Henry?" queried Mrs. Shannon.

"Special reason? What special reason?" demanded Mr. Shannon.

"Well—Dorothy!"

"Oh, that! I mean, her. Yes. Yes, that's very likely."

"She hasn't said anything yet. Not to me, at least. But then, you don't always, just at first. I remember—*we* didn't——"

Somebody knocked at the door. "Can I come in?" called Conrad. "Just," his mother called back.

Conrad had come to say good-night. It was quite a superfluous proceeding, but he was tremendously sentimental (although he would have denied it hotly if you had asserted it), and he hated going to bed without satisfying himself that there was no trouble anywhere. The reason he gave, however, as he appeared in the doorway was entirely different.

"Five-eighths of the gold is removed, O Parents," he proclaimed, "and I thought you might like to see your scion in his right pyjamas before going to sleep."

His eternal banter was his reply to his sentiment.

"You are a silly!" laughed Mrs. Shannon. "But wasn't it fun?"

"Rather! Did you enjoy it, Mother?"

"Every moment!"

"I won't ask *you*, Dad," grinned the boy. "I counted your winks. You just missed your century!"

"You know what *you* want, my boy," retorted Mr. Shannon. "A smack in the pants!"

He grinned back ferociously.

Half a minute later, Conrad was knocking on Dorothy's door, but he poked his head in this time without waiting for permission.

"That was very naughty of you!" exclaimed Dorothy. "I might have been anyhow!"

"You are anyhow," he replied, "and you don't excite me in the least. My mind is full of other women. I say, Sis, do you spend your entire life before your mirror?"

"Do slope off," she answered. "It's a bit late for brilliance!"

"I'm going. I only came to say good-night. It's a good, old-fashioned idea."

"Well, good-night."

"Good-night. Oh, just one question. *Was* I right?"

"When?"

"To be precise, eight hours ago?"

"What about?"

"About the only thing that matters in a young gell's life?"

She turned to him, with sudden color.

"Go away, go away, go away!" she exclaimed.

"I am answered," he retorted. "Though, as a

matter of fact, I knew. Until the last dance, Harold remained manly. Then he went all slush. Don't worry—I won't tell the old folks at home. I expect you want to do that yourself. But I may just say, though you won't believe it, that I'm so damned glad I could almost be sick. I think old Harold's a toff— and you ain't bad."

She rushed to him and flung her arms round him.

"There, now I'm all over face-cream," he muttered. "However, once in a lifetime!"

His last remark before going to sleep was made to his pillow.

"Would you mind informing me, sweetheart," he asked, "why I feel so peculiar and weepy?"

There was a tiny, dull glow in Sally's fireplace when she returned to her room. She dropped wearily into a chair and stared at it.

"What have *you* waited up for?" she asked. "Did you think I was bringing a friend home?"

The cynical question produced a sudden shudder. But for the gruesome turn of events, she might have brought a friend home with her, however unwillingly. The friend might have thrown himself down on her bed, just as she had thrown herself into this chair, and he might have been lying there at this moment, waiting. "Keep yer promise, Sally!" She heard the rough, unpleasant voice in her imagination, and in her imagination she answered it. "I didn't make any promise." "Yes, yer did." "No—I said 'perhaps.'" "Well, perhaps is as good as a promise to me. Come along—or must I make yer?"

And then? "I wonder if I've been damn lucky, after all?" she thought. For she *wouldn't* have come to him. She swore she wouldn't have! She had risen a cut above Sam! So there might have been a real hellish scrap. She might have—done anything!

The thought brought her head round. sharply to the bed, as though she feared to find the materialization of her vision. But the bed was empty. The man who might have lain there had harder substance beneath his back.

With a grating laugh she turned her head again to the dying embers.

"So what *are* you waiting up for?" she repeated. "It's all over bar the shouting!"

Then, all at once, she knew; and the knowledge made her laugh again.

She drew from her bosom a roll of films. Slowly and deliberately, as though fascinated by the process, she unwound the film, separating it from the red paper. When she had finished, the film and the paper made two separate coiling heaps on the floor. The paper heap had no value, but somewhere in the heap of film lay an undeveloped secret that, even now, might be worth a small fortune.

But Sally was not interested in the small fortune. She picked up the film and threw it on the dying fire.

It lay there for a moment motionless. Then it began to coil and sizzle. The next instant the sizzle rose to a tearing roar, the celluloid burst into hissing flames, and shadows leaped faintly along the glowing walls.

The flames died down.

"Well, that's that," she said. "And what's the next?"

She undressed, and stood naked before her mirror. Then she turned out the light and got into bed.

In another bed lay Warwick Hilling. Sally's bed was wide and yielding. Hilling's was narrow and lumpy, and had ugly black iron rails. And, also unlike Sally's, its occupant had not got into it unassisted. The Prince stood by its side.

"In a moment I must go," said the Prince. "Can you hear me?"

Hilling nodded feebly.

"Then listen, and remember all I say," continued the Prince, speaking slowly and clearly. "Bad things have happened. Things to grieve over. Things to re-

gret. But things, also, to forget. You will assist no
one by keeping them in your mind or by proclaim-
ing your knowledge. Indeed, to do so may raise issues
which will lead to a chaos you have no conception of,
and bring more death to the innocent. Of three who
have died tonight, one at least had a great spirit.
That great spirit asks you to continue your faith in
it, and not to undo the work for which it has died.
Do you understand all this? Do my words mean anything to you?"

Hilling nodded again. The words floated over him
like a strange, comforting blanket, removing a responsibility too big to be borne.

"But you are a man of intelligence," went on the
Prince, his voice growing fainter and fainter to the
man on the bed. "Your mind questions, and will
not be satisfied tomorrow with a mere instruction.
So I add this, though less for your intelligence than
for your conscience. What you have done—and what
I have done—these things have not been done for
selfish ends. They have been done for the great cause
of peace. Three people are dead to save the lives of
thousands, and you have helped to save the lives of
the thousands. When two of the three are found dead
together in the Albert Hall, it will be a good thing
for the world if the world thinks they have killed each
other. When the third is found dead in a lonely

house—no, if he is found there," the Prince corrected himself, after a moment's thought, "it will be good for the world if his death remains a mystery. Fortunately it is in the interest of all who know the truth to preserve silence. So your part, too, is silence."

The Prince was not sure whether he was heard this time. Warwick Hilling's eyes were closed, and he was breathing quietly. But he bent over the bed to conclude:

"In a few hours I shall return, and then, perhaps we can talk of other matters. A trip to the Continent, perhaps? I would like to show you my country, Mr. Hilling."

Then he stole softly to the door and left the room. The streets were still dark when he re-entered them and turned his steps westward, but the fog was clearing.

THE END

CPSIA information can be obtained at www.ICGtesting.com
Printed in the USA
LVOW07*1046040115

421434LV00003B/31/P

9 781258 071226